Cut of the Cards

Clint took out his gun and tried the door. It was unlocked.

The door opened soundlessly and the Gunsmith stepped inside. At first it looked dark but then he saw why. He was on one side of a wagon covered with a tarp, and there *was* a lamp lit, but it was on the other side.

It was then that he saw the man sitting on the ground. There was a lit storm lamp near him. His legs were spread out and he had a deck of cards dealt out between them.

"Red queen on black king," Clint said, stepping into view.

The man looked up quickly and started to reach for his holstered gun.

"Don't," the Gunsmith ordered.

The man froze.

Also in THE GUNSMITH series

MACKLIN'S WOMEN
THE CHINESE GUNMAN
THE WOMAN HUNT
THE GUNS OF ABILENE
THREE GUNS FOR GLORY
LEADTOWN
THE LONGHORN WAR
QUANAH'S REVENGE
HEAVYWEIGHT GUN
NEW ORLEANS FIRE
ONE-HANDED GUN
THE CANADIAN PAYROLL
DRAW TO AN INSIDE DEATH
DEAD MAN'S HAND
BANDIT GOLD
BUCKSKINS AND SIX-GUNS
SILVER WAR
HIGH NOON AT LANCASTER
BANDIDO BLOOD
EAGLE'S GAP
THE PONDEROSA WAR
TROUBLE RIDES A FAST HORSE
DYNAMITE JUSTICE
THE POSSE
NIGHT OF THE GILA
THE BOUNTY WOMEN
BLACK PEARL SALOON
GUNDOWN IN PARADISE
KING OF THE BORDER
THE EL PASO SALT WAR
THE TEN PINES KILLER
HELL WITH A PISTOL
THE WYOMING CATTLE KILL
THE GOLDEN HORSEMAN
THE SCARLET GUN
NAVAHO DEVIL
WILD BILL'S GHOST
THE MINER'S SHOWDOWN
ARCHER'S REVENGE
SHOWDOWN IN RATON
WHEN LEGENDS MEET
DESERT HELL
THE DIAMOND GUN
DENVER DUO
HELL ON WHEELS
THE LEGEND MAKER
WALKING DEAD MAN
CROSSFIRE MOUNTAIN
THE DEADLY HEALER
THE TRAIL DRIVE WAR
GERONIMO'S TRAIL
THE COMSTOCK GOLD FRAUD
BOOMTOWN KILLER
TEXAS TRACKDOWN
THE FAST DRAW LEAGUE
SHOWDOWN IN RIO MALO
OUTLAW TRAIL
HOMESTEADER GUNS
FIVE CARD DEATH
TRAILDRIVE TO MONTANA
TRIAL BY FIRE
THE OLD WHISTLER GANG
DAUGHTER OF GOLD
APACHE GOLD
PLAINS MURDER
DEADLY MEMORIES
THE NEVADA TIMBER WAR
NEW MEXICO SHOWDOWN
BARBED WIRE AND BULLETS
DEATH EXPRESS
WHEN LEGENDS DIE
SIXGUN JUSTICE
MUSTANG HUNTERS
TEXAS RANSOM
VENGEANCE TOWN
WINNER TAKE ALL
MESSAGE FROM A DEAD MAN
RIDE FOR VENGEANCE
THE TAKERSVILLE SHOOT
BLOOD ON THE LAND
SIXGUN SHOWDOWN
MISSISSIPPI MASSACRE
THE ARIZONA TRIANGLE
BROTHERS OF THE GUN
THE STAGECOACH THIEVES
JUDGMENT AT FIRECREEK
DEAD MAN'S JURY
HANDS OF THE STRANGLER
NEVADA DEATH TRAP
WAGON TRAIN TO HELL

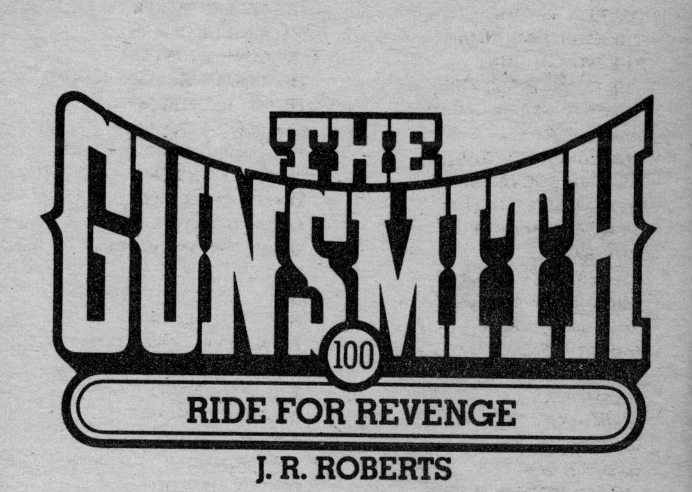

J. R. ROBERTS

JOVE BOOKS, NEW YORK

RIDE FOR REVENGE

A Jove Book/published by arrangement with
the author

PRINTING HISTORY
Jove edition/April 1990

ISBN: 0-515-10288-1

Jove Books are published by The Berkley Publishing Group,
200 Madison Avenue, New York, New York 10016.

PRINTED IN THE UNITED STATES OF AMERICA

10 9 8 7 6 5 4 3 2 1

This book is dedicated to
the Gunsmith readers
for helping us to our first centennial.

PROLOGUE

I

There was a time when things were simpler.

That was a long time ago, Clint Adams thought, before he became known as the Gunsmith.

Before he became a target for every would-be legend of the West who thought he was hell-on-wheels with a gun . . . like Hoke Winston.

Clint had first run into Winston in Red Sand, New Mexico. Winston, probably all of twenty years old, backed *and* egged on by two buddies, had approached Clint's table in the Silver Eagle Saloon. . . .

"You the Gunsmith?"

Clint looked up from his beer and stared at the younger man.

"My name is Clint Adams, son."

Winston turned, looked at his friends, and then turned back.

"Yeah, that's what I said," he said. "Clint Adams, the Gunsmith."

"What is it you want, son?"

"You," Winston said, "out in the street."

"For what?"

Winston frowned at the question and said, "You know."

"No, I don't know," Clint said. "Suppose you tell me." He had gone through this hundreds of times before. He was sure even some of the dialogue was the same. He was sure that Hickok, and Ben Thompson, and Wyatt Earp, and many others had been through the same without much change in the dialogue.

"We're gonna have us a shoot-out!" the boy said seriously.

Clint stared at Winston for a few moments before he burst out laughing.

"A shoot-out?" he repeated to the confused-looking young man. "Son, you've been reading too many damned dime novels."

The boy's face reddened and he said, "Stop calling me 'son.'"

Clint stopped laughing and said, "Suppose you tell me your name, so I know what to call you."

"My name's Hoke Winston."

"Well, Mr. Winston," Clint said, "if I offended you by calling you 'son,' I apologize."

"Apologize?"

That *really* confused Hoke Winston. He frowned, turned and looked at his friends, and then turned back. Suddenly his face lit up, as if everything had become clear to him.

"Oh, I get it," Winston said, smiling now. "You're yeller."

"Well," Clint said, "if believing that will make you go away, then sure, I'm yeller."

"You don't wanna meet me in the street!" Winston accused.

"That's right, Hoke," Clint said, "I don't."

Winston couldn't understand it. His remarks were designed to bring the man out of his chair, ready to fight.

"You don't care if all these people think you're yeller?" Winston asked.

"Nope."

"What kind of man are you?"

"I'm alive," Clint said, "and I didn't get this way going out into the street with every hothead who wants me there."

"Who you callin' a 'hothead'?" Winston wasn't even

sure what it meant, but he knew it wasn't good.

"You, Hoke Winston," Clint said. "If I was you I'd turn around now and walk out while you can."

Winston was about to turn to look at his friends, but Clint said, "Don't look at them. They pushed you into this, but they aren't going to back you. You're on your own."

Winston stared at Clint hard, firmed his jaw, and asked, "Are you coming outside?"

"No, I am not."

"Then I'll have to try you here," Winston said, and he spread his legs.

"Don't, Hoke," Clint warned. "My gun is already out."

Winston froze. "Where?"

"Under the table."

Winston stared at Clint and said, "It ain't."

"Touch your gun and find out," Clint said.

Winston remained frozen, wishing he had the nerve to lean over and look under the table.

"Turn around, walk out, and live," Clint said.

"You're making a fool out of me," Winston said.

Clint shook his head. "You did that to yourself," he said. "I'm trying to keep you alive."

Winston took a step back, then stopped and said, "I ain't gonna forget this, Adams."

"Good," Clint said, "I don't want you to."

Winston backed up all the way to the door of the saloon, then turned and walked out. His two friends hastily followed. Clint removed his empty right hand from beneath the table.

That was the end of it.

He thought. . . .

Just moments before he had been riding Duke through a gully about five miles out of Red Sand when he heard the shot just a split second before he felt the impact of the bullet. It struck him in the upper portion of his right arm, where it joined the shoulder.

He leaped instinctively from Duke's back and hit the ground rolling, alert for the sound of a second shot. He came to a stop on his left side in the gully and lay still. He figured that if the bushwhacker thought he was dead, he'd either ride away or come walking up.

It didn't happen that way.

In fact, *nothing* happened for about ten minutes, and then Clint had to move because of the pain. As soon as he moved, there was another shot. Clint looked around, saw a large boulder, and scrambled over to it.

That's where he was now, seated with his back against that rock. He knew he'd been hit bad because he couldn't move his right arm. He'd had to reach across his body and take his gun out of his holster with his left hand.

He was almost certain that the bushwhacker was Hoke Winston.

He sat with his wound pressed against the stone, hoping that would stop the bleeding long enough for him to decide his next move.

He just needed a minute. . . .

II

Clint Adams was twenty-five years old and back in the town of Stratton, in the Oklahoma Territory. He was a deputy sheriff who had recently begun working on his own guns. He had worked his way West from the East and become fascinated with guns along the way. In the eighteen months he'd been settled in Stratton he had worked with his gun, learning not only *how* to use it, but *how* it worked.

What he found out was that he had a natural ability with the weapon. He could hit what he aimed at almost every time, and with practice he knew he would become even better. Also, he had taken the gun apart and put it together again countless times, and now he was beginning to do the same with other guns. In fact, the town gunsmith, Deke Henry, allowed him to come into the shop and work on any gun he liked. Henry made no attempts to *teach* Adams anything. He was a gunsmith, not a gunman. He built them and repaired them, but he did not himself use them.

As a twenty-five-year-old deputy, just beginning to realize what he could do with a gun, Clint Adams had no idea that he would someday become the legendary Gunsmith, a target for every hothead who thought he was good with a gun.

Like Hoke Winston . . .

". . . Hoke Winston!"

Clint came awake with a start. He was no longer twenty-five years old and in Stratton; he was here, very likely bleeding to death, and if he drifted off to sleep again he probably *would* bleed to death.

What had awakened him?

"Did you hear me, Adams?" a voice called. "This is Hoke Winston!"

"Winston . . ." Clint said, but it came out a whisper. He thought about his canteen and wondered how far Duke had gone with it. He could use some water just about now.

"I told you I wouldn't forget what happened in that saloon, Adams!" Winston called out. "You're hurt bad, ain't you?"

That was true. He was hurt real bad, and he had to do something about it.

He put his gun down and pulled his handkerchief out of his pocket. Balling it up, he reached around with his left hand and slid the cloth beneath his shirt, pressing it against the wound. He hissed at the pain his movements caused and then leaned back against the rock again, wedging the cloth against the wound. He picked up the gun again and tried to control his breathing. If he was going to get out of this he was going to have to keep his wits about him. He was going to have to keep himself from drifting off again.

Jesus, he thought, Stratton was a long way off. He hadn't thought about that time in a long while, and now wasn't the time to start reminiscing. . . .

Her name was Jennifer Sand and she was twenty years old. She had long red hair, an upturned nose, and a wide, full-lipped mouth. He had been thinking about asking her to marry him when Harve Bennett rode into Stratton and gunned down old Jim Bailey, the sheriff. Clint felt it was his responsibility to hunt Harve Bennett down and bring him to justice, but Jenny Sand felt differently. She told Clint that if he left to track Bennett, she would not be there when he got back—and she kept her word. They had met again thirteen years later, but circumstances had kept them from rekindling the flame.

Clint had left Stratton after that to travel and had taken jobs along the way as deputy sheriff, sheriff, marshal, building his reputation as a lawman and as a fast hand with a gun. He was still working on guns along the way, until he'd finally reworked his single-action Colt, modifying it so that it was a *double*-action Colt. When the word on that got out, some smart small-time reporter did a story on him, calling him the ''Gunsmith'' for the first time. The story was picked by larger newspapers throughout the West and by some dime novelists in the East, and the legend of the Gunsmith—a legend to rival even that of Wild Bill Hickok—was born. . . .

Jesus, he thought as he came awake, I did it again. He rubbed his left hand over his face. Winston and his friends could have ridden down on him with no problem if they'd known he was asleep—or passed out.

He felt hot, the kind of heat that crept down behind the eyes and became a fever. If he was running a fever he was going to *have* to make a move or risk passing out and *not* waking up.

He picked his gun up in his left hand and hefted it. He could use the gun with his left hand—not as accurately as with his right, but well enough to handle a Hoke Winston and his two friends. All he had to do was get to his feet. . . .

Clint Adams was in his midthirties, and prepared to give up the life of a lawman. He'd had several thankless jobs as a town sheriff, cleaning up the towns and then falling prey to the town councils, who felt they had no need of a fast-gun, big-rep lawman anymore. He was tired of being used by those kinds of people—town builders, people users.

By then his reputation was widespread. He was well known as a lawman, better known as a man with a gun—

a man with a reputation as big as Wild Bill Hickok's. He was unhappy with it, because others were constantly looking to try him. He wasn't afraid of them, but he *was* tired of the killing. Things were going to change.

An accomplished gunsmith, he decided to outfit a wagon, buy a team, and start to travel, plying a trade not as "the" Gunsmith but as "a" gunsmith.

His hope was that he would be able to live a normal life from then on, staying away from trouble and away from the reputation hunters. What he found was that, whether he liked it or not, he was there for people who were in trouble, and the world was full of them. He also found that there was no way to escape who he was, who others *saw* him as—the Gunsmith.

The Gunsmith . . .

"Hey, Gunsmith?"

Coming awake—*again*—Clint Adams knew that he owed his life to his reputation. If he *weren't* the Gunsmith, Winston and his friends would have come for him by now. They were probably either waiting for him to bleed to death or to become so weak that they could just walk up on him and kill him. That was odd, he thought. Men had tried him before, and had tried to *kill* him before, but it was odd for a man who thought he was good enough to *face* the Gunsmith to turn around and decide to bushwhack him. Hoke Winston had obviously been shaken by their encounter in the saloon, to the point where he now no longer worried about *how* he would kill the Gunsmith, just that he kill him.

And if the great legend didn't get to his feet *now*, Winston and his friends would do just that.

III

"Gunsmith!" Hoke Winston called. "Are you alive down there?"

Clint was about to answer, but that would have been a show of pure bravado. He thought better of it. Let them go on guessing.

He decided it was time to get to his feet, lest he pass out again. He never remembered passing out, only waking up—and he wanted to live to do both again.

He pulled his legs up under him first, then braced his back against the rock and painfully rose to his feet. He tried to ignore the fact that while his shoulder burned with pain, his right arm felt numb. If his arm were permanently damaged—but he only had that to worry about if he lived, so he might as well take care of *that* little matter first.

He was on his feet—none too steady, but upright nevertheless. He wiped the sweat from his brow with the back of his left hand before it could fall into his eyes, then slid the gun into his belt, dried his left hand on his pants, and palmed the gun again.

He moved away from the rock and risked a look around it. He couldn't see anything; he didn't know where Winston and his friends were. Under normal circumstances, he would wait them out, wait for them to reveal themselves, but these circumstances were far from normal. He was going to have to *draw* them out, and there was only one thing he had that would do that.

Himself.

"Winston!"

"That you, Gunsmith?"

Clint hoped that his voice sounded strong and steady enough.

"You're a bad shot, Winston."

There was a pause, and then Winston said, "Oh no, Adams. I *saw* you hit."

"You think so?"

"I know so."

"Then let's do it, Winston," Clint said. "Let's do what you wanted to do in town. Right here, right now. Just you and me."

There was no reply.

"What are you worried about, Hoke?" Clint called. "If I'm wounded, you have the edge you need."

"I don't need an edge to take you, Adams!"

"Tell that to your friends, Hoke," Clint said, "but I think they'll want to see it to believe it."

Clint could imagine Winston's two friends looking at him now, waiting to see if he would take up the challenge from what they all felt was a wounded Gunsmith. Under that kind of pressure, Winston would have to agree.

Clint had one advantage: His wound was in the back, and Winston and his friends wouldn't be able to see the blood. He slid his gun back into his holster, butt out, set for a left-handed draw, and waited.

Hoke Winston could feel the eyes of his friends, Wayne McQueen and Bob Lansing, burning into his back. He bit his lip and replayed the shooting in his mind. He was *sure* that he'd hit Adams, who must have been running a bluff.

"What are you gonna do, Hoke?" McQueen asked.

"What do you think?" Winston answered without turning around. "I'm going to kill the Gunsmith, just like I planned."

"Are we gonna do this, Hoke?" Clint called out.

There was a moment's hesitation, then Winston's voice called out, "All right, Adams. Let's do it. Who steps out first?"

Clint thought for a moment and then said, "We'll step out together. Have one of your partners count to three." If either of them can, he added to himself.

Moments later a quavering voice called out, "One . . . two . . . three!"

Clint stepped out, hoping he wouldn't fall on his face. He was prepared to find himself facing all three men instead of just Winston. He was prepared to do that because even if he didn't, he'd die soon anyway from his wound. As it turned out, Hoke Winston *had* stepped out by himself, and the two men stared at each other.

Clint knew he was drenched with sweat from the wound and the fever it had brought on, but it was hot enough so that Winston was also soaking.

Both men knew they were too far away and instinctively began walking toward each other. Clint stopped when he was able to see the look on Winston's face and in his eyes clearly.

Winston took a couple of extra steps and then stopped abruptly.

"Let's get it over with, Hoke," Clint said. "I've got other things to do."

"You—" Winston said, taunted for the last time.

Both men reached for their guns at the same time, Clint's left hand reaching across his body and grasping the reversed butt.

Winston's hand was coming up with his gun at the same time. The younger man's move was good, but Clint knew that if he were uninjured he would have killed the man easily.

As it was, both men fired at the same time. Winston's shot was rushed, and it went wide. Clint's shot was much more deliberate. The bullet struck Winston squarely in the chest, staggering him back a step or two and bringing a shocked look to his face.

As Hoke Winston fell forward, all of the strength seemed to go out of Clint Adams's body, and he felt himself falling as well. . . .

IV

When Clint awoke he was aware of the feel of cool, crisp sheets. He lay there for a moment, taking stock of himself. For a moment he was afraid to look, for fear that it wouldn't be there, but when he finally sneaked a glance he saw it.

He still had his right arm.

He waited a moment while the relief flooded over him, then he lifted his head to check out his surroundings.

It looked as if he were in a small cabin, or at least one small room in a cabin. His mouth was very dry, and his arm itched, but that didn't bother him. He was glad it itched because that reminded him that it was still there.

He did want to quench his thirst, though.

He saw a pitcher on top of a scarred dresser across the room, and on the off chance that it contained water he threw the sheets back with the intention of walking over there.

His mind was willing, but that's about the only part of him that was. He was about to try to rise again when the door opened and a woman walked in.

"What in tarnation!" she said, staring at him.

"Water," he tried to say, but it came out a dry croak.

Using his left arm, he pointed to the pitcher on the dresser top.

"You want water?" she asked.

He nodded.

"Well, get back in bed there, and I'll get it for ya," she said.

He started to ease himself back down but found he couldn't hold himself. He fell onto his back, his head on the pillow, and waited there for her to come with the water.

"Here ya go," she said.

She slid her hand beneath his head, to the back of his neck, and lifted him enough so that he could drink from the tin cup she was holding. She appeared to be tall and slender, but he was aware of surprising strength in her hands.

He sipped the water, and although it wasn't cool, it was wet, and that's what counted.

"Thanks," he said, as she let his head back down.

"You're welcome," she said, setting aside the tin cup. "I'm glad to see that you was tryin' to get up. In fact, I'm glad to see you awake."

"How long have I been here?"

"Better part of a week."

"A week?"

"That's right."

"How'd I get here?"

"I brung you."

"You?"

She nodded.

"Found you lying near a dead man, pretty near dead yourself. I hauled you up on my horse and brought you back here. You been here since."

"Was there . . . a doctor?" he asked, pausing to moisten his lips with his tongue and swallow.

"Hell, ain't a doctor for miles," she said, "but I done enough doctorin' in my time."

"I appreciate what you did for me."

"I was gonna take that arm from ya," she said, matter-of-factly, "but seein' the kind of man you was, I didn't think you'd thank me for that. Figured you'd rather be dead than crippled."

"The kind of man I am?"

"Killed that feller, didn't you?"

"Yes."

"For the price on his head?"

"No."

"Why then?"

Clint told her why, and when he was finished with his story his mouth was dry again. She gave him another drink.

"My horse?"

"A big black brute?"

"That's him."

"Found him the same day I found you. He's fine."

"What, uh, happened to Winston?"

"The dead man?"

"Yes."

"I left him where he lay. I reckon his two friends must have run off in a hurry—too much of a hurry to take him or to kill you. Must have been a cowardly pair, too scared to check and see if you was alive."

"They bushwhacked me," Clint said. "I guess that makes them cowards."

"I guess I agree," she said. "You'd better rest up some, this being your first day awake and all. You'll be here awhile, healin' up."

"I don't want to be in your way."

"T'ain't," she said. "Every once in a while I kin use the company. You play checkers?"

"Yes."

"Well, when you get some of your strength back we can have us some games."

"Fine."

"I'll go and fix some soup. You'll be able to eat some later."

"Thanks."

She walked to the door, then turned back and asked, "What's your name?"

"Clint."

"Clint, I'm Mae. Just so we know who's who."

Clint wanted to nod, but by then he'd fallen back to sleep.

Clint dreamed a lot after that, mostly about his past. He must have dreamed the first week he was there, as well, but he didn't remember those.

He dreamed about old friends like Bat Masterson and Wyatt Earp and Wild Bill Hickok; he dreamed about men he knew but wasn't sure he could actually call friends, like Luke Short and Ben Thompson; he also dreamed about women, like Anne Archer, a lady bounty hunter he had become *very* fond of over the past couple of years; and Joanna Morgan, a woman he had almost married, who had been killed up north in Alaska.

He dreamed about times before he was the Gunsmith and times after, and he wasn't sure which times he preferred. Things were certainly simpler before, but he'd never really had an identity then. There were times when he'd wished he didn't *have* the rep as the Gunsmith, but of late he'd sort of come to terms with his reputation. He no longer hated it, but he still wasn't sure he liked it.

What he was doing these days, more often than not, was living with it.

He woke up and became aware of the weight on his left arm. He turned his head and saw Mae asleep atop it.

He certainly hadn't any idea that she was going to end up in bed with him, but after they had played checkers for four days, she came into the room the fifth night without the checkerboard.

"No game tonight?" he asked.

"You're getting stronger," she said. "I thought we might as well play something else tonight."

It surprised him. She had not given any indication that she was thinking about this. She opened her threadbare robe, the same robe she had worn the last four nights while they played checkers, and dropped it to the floor.

Her body surprised him. She was tall and slender, but her breasts were larger and firmer than he would have thought. She was a hard worker, and it showed in the muscles of her upper arms and her thighs. It also showed on her face, which bore lines that belied her age. He had guessed her to be forty and found out later that she was six years younger. Her belly was flat and her hips were somewhat bony, but her breasts and the smoothness of her skin were a pleasant surprise. He felt his body reacting beneath the bedclothes.

She grew uncomfortable beneath his stare and said, "I could always go and get the checkerboard."

He threw back the sheet and said, "Shut up and get in, Mae."

She was eager, and if she was not inexperienced, she was somewhat out of practice. As he kissed her breasts and sucked her nipples, he felt her shudder beneath him and then sigh. He mounted her then, entering her slowly, and he had to reach beneath her and cup her slim buttocks to slow her down. He controlled the tempo, taking her in deep, slow strokes. Her breath began to come in rasps as she clutched at him, speaking to him and telling him "Yes!" and "Oh!" and "Oh God!" over and over until he felt her belly begin to tremble and knew she was teetering on the edge. . . .

Three days later he was well enough to sit a horse and leave.

"You take care of yerself, Clint," Mae said as he mounted up outside her front door.

"I will, Mae."

"Don't go messing with all the work I done to keep you alive."

"I won't."

"And come back and see a woman once in a while," she said, smiling. "I ain't found a sucker at checkers like you in a long time."

ONE

Talbot Roper knew he was being followed.

He hadn't seen anybody, and he hadn't even really *heard* anyone, but he knew that someone was behind him, dogging his trail.

Roper prided himself on being able to adapt himself to whatever terrain he happened to be working in; whether he was in the desert, or the mountains, or horse country, or Indian country, it didn't matter to him. He was a private detective, but he had been a lot of things over the years and had lived in a lot of different places. It was precisely this that enabled him to be as good a detective as he was.

He was in Denver now, though, and this was *his* terrain, this was where he belonged, and he was annoyed—no, he was *angry*—that someone thought they could tail him and he wouldn't know it.

He decided to take his tail on a little tour.

Kit's was a restaurant that catered to a very special clientele. The food was expensive and delicious and the entertainment was first rate. They had a bar, but it was not open to the general public. Talbot Roper was one of the few people who could walk into the bar at Kit's any time he wanted to.

That was because he knew Kit.

Very well!

Kit was Kit Russell. She owned Kit's and on occasion even sang at Kit's.

As Roper entered the restaurant, the doorman recognized him right away.

"Mr. Roper, how nice to see you."

The doorman was Dutch Mantle, and he was big enough to also be the bouncer—but he wasn't. Dutch's brother Maurice was the bouncer. Dutch and Maurice were identical twins, but for some reason Dutch looked better in a tuxedo—as well as a man who is six-foot-six can look in a tuxedo.

"Hello, Dutch. Is Miss Russell in?"

"Yes, sir. She's in her office at the moment. Shall I send for her?"

"No, I'll go to her office."

"Will you be dining with us tonight?"

"I don't think so."

Roper turned and looked back out the door.

"Is something wrong, sir?"

"Dutch, I believe there's a man following me."

"I see. Would you like to have me send Maurice—"

"No, no, nothing like that. I'd just like to know if someone tries to get in here after me."

"I see," Dutch said. "Well, I can certainly handle that, Mr. Roper."

"Thanks, Dutch."

"Of course, sir."

"Oh, uh, is there any action tonight?"

"Yes, sir," Dutch said, and he didn't elaborate because he didn't have to elaborate. Roper knew that Kit had some rooms in the back that she leased on occasion for certain . . . games of chance. Roper just wanted to know what he was walking into.

"All right, Dutch, thanks."

Dutch nodded and looked past Roper as an obviously wealthy couple entered.

Roper walked through the restaurant, in which there was

not an empty table, and went to the bar past Walter, the man whose job it was to keep people away from the bar. Walter didn't speak to Roper, but he knew who he was and so allowed him to enter. Walter was Dutch and Maurice's cousin—their *smaller* cousin, as he was only six-four.

The bar was crowded, which meant that there were a lot of men present who were *perceived* as being important. In point of fact, Roper recognized many of the people who were there—from the worlds of law, and politics, and the theater—and he was less than impressed with most of them. To be fair, they probably felt the same way about him.

He found a space at the bar and waved at the bartender, an ex-prizefighter named Max.

"Mr. Roper, boy, am I glad to see you," Max said, coming over and pumping Roper's hand.

"Why so glad, Max?"

"You see the crowd we got tonight?" Max said, spreading his huge hands. "A bunch of phonies. It's nice to see somebody real for a change."

"Well, how about a real beer then?" Roper asked.

"Coming up."

Max drew Roper a cold beer and barely had time to serve it to him when he was called to another part of the bar.

Roper was nursing his beer, wondering if he should go back out the front way or use a back exit to get *behind* whoever was tailing him.

Roper had just become involved in a very important case, and the fact that he was being followed that night could not have been a coincidence, as far as he was concerned. He decided that he would use the rear exit and get the drop on his tail and find out who he was and why he was following him.

He had just finished his beer and was about to make his way to the rear exit when he felt a hand on his shoulder—a huge hand.

He turned and found himself looking up at Maurice Mantle, Dutch's brother.

"Maurice, hello," he said.

"Miss Russell sent me to ask you to come to her office, Mr. Roper," Maurice said. He was not as well spoken as his brother, but he usually managed to get his point across.

Roper hesitated a moment, then decided that it couldn't do any harm to go and see Kit.

Later he would realize how wrong he was.

"All right, Maurice," he said, "lead the way."

Maurice led Roper to the door of Kit Russell's second-floor office and stopped there. Roper knocked and entered, leaving Maurice outside.

Kit Russell was twenty-five, although one would have thought her more mature than that by her demeanor. She was a statuesque, creamy-skinned, red-haired woman who could have laid legitimate claim to being the most beautiful woman in Denver if her ego needed that kind of thing—which it didn't. For a woman so young she was extremely wise in the ways of the world *and* in business, and she carried herself with extreme confidence when it came to any aspect of her life.

Except when it came to Talbot Roper.

When it came to Roper she was unsure of her position. They had been friends and they had been lovers, but while she would have preferred to be more of the latter, he appeared satisfied being more of the former.

She was sitting behind her desk when Roper entered, apparently engrossed in paperwork. He closed the door and stood there looking at her. She was wearing green that night, a wonderful color for her, and he admired her while he waited for her to finish what she was doing.

She looked up at him finally and said, "I heard you were here."

"Just for a little while."

"I haven't seen you for a while," she said. "Did you intend to say hello?"

He saw then that she was angry.

"I'm involved in something, Kit."

"Something which kept you from coming up and saying hello?"

"Kit—"

"All right," she said, "never mind. I'm being silly. There's no rule that says you *have* to come up and say hello *every* time you come here. I should understand that."

She stood up then, and he saw that her green gown reached to the floor and covered her to the neck. If she had been standing next to another woman, however, who was wearing something low cut and short, she would still have commanded more attention. She had full breasts and wide shoulders, and he knew that beneath that gown she had the longest, smoothest legs in Denver.

"I have work to do," she said. "I'll be back up here in about twenty minutes, if you care to stay."

"Kit . . . I'm going to use the rear exit."

She glared at him. He knew he had been neglecting her of late, but he didn't feel prepared at that moment to explain why.

"I'm sorry," he said, lamely. "I'm . . . involved in something—"

"So you mentioned," she said, interrupting him. "I guess neither one of us has the time to talk now." She opened the door and added, "You let me know when you do, all right?"

"Kit—"

She opened the door and walked out.

There was a door behind her desk, which led to a stairway that went down to the rear door. Roper didn't want to lose the man who was following him, so he didn't have the time to go after Kit Russell and try and explain himself. He crossed the room and went through the door and down the stairs to the rear exit. He was still thinking about Kit Russell when he went through the door, as well as the man who was waiting for him to come out of the restaurant out front so he could continue to tail him.

He was in the dark alley behind the restaurant, surrounded by trash bins and crates. He started to work his way through and around them when he heard a sound behind him. He was in the act of turning when he heard the shot. He felt searing, white-hot pain and he saw the flash of the second shot before everything faded away into black.

TWO

The telegram found Clint Adams in Labyrinth, Texas, his home away from the trail.

In fact, Clint had been thinking about that for a few days—the fact that when he wasn't on the trail he always seemed to be in Labyrinth. Maybe he should just settle down there once and for all—but every time he thought that way he could feel his feet itching to move again.

So he came to Labyrinth when the trail ate away the soles of his shoes and he needed to rest for a while. Although he kept himself apart from the rest of the townspeople, they all knew who he was. He did have one good friend there—Rick Hartman, who owned Rick's Place, the biggest saloon and gambling house in town.

He was sitting in Rick's with Rick when the kid came in with the telegram. He saw the kid enter, and when the boy started for him he said to Rick, "Now *this* is never good news."

Rick turned and saw the kid approaching their table, holding a yellow piece of paper in his hand.

"Maybe it's not for you," he said.

Clint sipped his beer and said, "It's for me, all right. I can feel it."

The kid reached the table and said, "It's for you, Mr. Gunsmith," holding it out to him.

Clint grimaced at Rick, accepted the telegram, and tossed the kid two bits.

"Thanks," the boy said, and he ran off.

Rick remained silent while Clint read the telegram, trying in vain to read the expression on his friend's face.

"So?" he asked, finally. "How bad is *bad*?"

"Remember Talbot Roper?" Clint asked.

"I've never met him, but I know who he is. He used to be a Pinkerton before he left to open his own agency. He's based in Denver, isn't he?"

"Yes, and that's where this telegram originated."

"Denver?"

"From Roper."

"The way I heard it, he's the best there is. What does he need, help?" Rick was joking.

"As a matter of fact," Clint said, "he does."

Clint handed the telegram to Rick, who read it:

CLINT ADAMS

COULD USE YOUR HELP. COULD YOU USE A LOT OF MONEY? COME TO DENVER—QUICKLY.

ROPER

"This doesn't sound like an urgent plea for help, does it?" Rick asked, handing the telegram back.

"It wouldn't—unless you knew Roper."

"And you do, so what does it mean?"

"See where he mentions money?"

"I see where he mentioned a *lot* of money," Rick said.

"Well, that makes it an urgent plea," Clint said. "Roper has never split a fee, let alone promised somebody a lot of money. Something must be wrong."

"If something is wrong, why didn't he just say so?"

"That's not what Tal would do," Clint said. "He wants me to come because he asked me to, not because he needs me to."

"Just how friendly are the two of you?"

"We respect each other."

"And that's why you're going to go?"

"No," Clint said, standing up, "I'm going to go because I'm curious, and that sonofabitch *knows* that."

Clint went to his hotel room to pack. He hadn't told Rick, but he was worried. He had gotten telegrams from Roper before, some asking him to come to Denver and become his partner, but he'd never gotten a summons like this. Something had to really be wrong for Roper to send for him and promise him money.

While he was packing, there was a knock at his door. He opened it and saw Glenna standing in the hallway.

"Are you going to ask me inside?" she asked.

"Sure," he said, moving aside so she could enter. "Come on in."

Each time he was away from Labyrinth and returned, he would find new girls working for Rick. Saloon girl was a transitory job, at best. Most girls took it to save a few dollars so they could move on to the next place. When he had returned this time, he found Glenna working there.

Glenna was of medium height and slender, with straight blond hair and eyes like a cat. They had noticed each other the first night he returned, and since they were both liable to pull up stakes at a moment's notice, they didn't waste any time.

She moved into his arms and he kissed her. Her mouth was yielding beneath his, soft and pliable. He'd noticed that she would kiss for as long or short a time as he wanted, and the same went for sex. She would spend as much or as little time in bed with him as he wanted. He'd never met a woman so willing—not eager, so much, but willing—to please a man.

"I heard you were leaving," she said.

"Tomorrow morning."

"For where?"

"Denver."

He walked to the bed and continued to pack.

"Hmm, I've never been to Denver."

He wasn't sure if that was a hint for an invitation, but if it was he didn't rise to the bait.

"Well," she said, "I came over to say good-bye."

"It's early," he said, turning to her. "We have plenty of time."

She moved to the bed, knelt on it, and swept his bag off of it onto the floor.

"The earlier we start," she said, "the more time we can take doing it."

They took their time and then went out for dinner.

"Don't you have to work tonight?" he asked.

"Yes," she said, "but I don't have to start until late. After that I could come to your room, if you like."

"To say good-bye some more?" he asked.

She smiled at him and said, "We can keep doing it until we get it right."

"That sounds fine to me."

In the morning Clint left Glenna asleep in his bed. He could have awoken her and said good-bye, but what would have been the point? They'd spent all night saying good-bye, so what was the point of one more moment in the morning? By the time he returned she'd be gone anyway, and they'd never see each other again.

He found a surprise waiting for him when he got to the livery stable.

"I don't believe my eyes," he said. "What are you doing up this early?"

Rick Hartman smiled and said, "I just thought I'd see you off."

"Well, that was nice of you," Clint said.

Rick went inside with Clint and watched while he saddled Duke.

"Leaving the rig behind?"

"I want to be able to travel fast," Clint said. "Besides, I'll be switching to the railroad soon and there's no room on a train for a team and rig."

"Just Duke, eh?"

Clint patted Duke's neck and led him outside.

"I have a feeling I'll be needing ol' Duke," Clint said. His affection for the big black gelding was plain in his tone.

"He is getting a little long in the tooth, isn't he?" Rick said.

"That's not what I meant," Clint said. "Duke can still outrun any colt half his age."

"Hey, you don't have to convince me," Rick said. "I'd bet on him."

Clint turned to him and stuck out his hand. "Well, I'll be seeing you."

"Soon, I hope," Rick said.

Clint looked into Rick's eyes and said, "Have you got something on your mind, Rick?"

"I—well, I do actually, yeah," Rick admitted.

"What?"

Rick hesitated a moment, then said, "I'd just like you to be extra careful on this."

Clint frowned. "Why?"

"I don't know why, Clint," Rick said. "I . . . just have this feeling that you're in for more than you might think."

"I don't know *what* I'm in for," Clint said, "so that might be saying a lot."

"Just watch your step."

"I always do, Rick," Clint said. He mounted up, then looked down at his friend and repeated, "I always do."

THREE

Clint had been to Denver before, several times. Most of the times he'd been there he'd been involved in one adventure or another. He had some acquaintances there, including Allan Pinkerton, and he had two friends there. One was Talbot Roper, who had almost always managed to be away on one case or another when Clint was in town.

The other friend was Ellie Lennox, the pretty Pinkerton detective he'd met a couple of years before.*

Before he'd boarded his train he had sent a telegram to Ellie, telling her that he was coming to Denver. He spotted her as soon as he stepped off the train, and she him.

Ellie waved and ran to him, straight into his arms. He had to drop his bag in order to catch her.

"Clint, how wonderful!" she said, kissing him. "I was so happy when I got your telegram."

"You look wonderful, Ellie."

And she did. Her dark hair was longer than he ever remembered.

"You've let your hair grow."

"You noticed," she said, pleased. "Come on, I'll take you to your hotel."

**THE GUNSMITH #53*

"I've got to make arrangements for Duke, and then we can go."

"All right. I'll go and bring the carriage around to the front of the station."

"I'll meet you there."

She gave him a quick kiss on the cheek and then ran off to get the carriage.

When Clint exited the station, Ellie was there with a carriage.

"Denver House?" she asked.

"Where else?"

She told the driver where to take them and then sat back next to Clint.

"As much as I'd like to believe it, I don't think you came here just to see me."

"Uh, no, I didn't," Clint admitted. "I got a telegram from Talbot Roper."

"The Great Detective?" she said, laughing.

"Is that what you call him?"

"That's what everyone in the business calls him, but I've got something to tell you."

She stopped short.

"What is it?"

"Well, maybe I should let him tell you, but it might be awhile."

"Why?"

"You don't know?"

"Know what?"

"He was shot."

"When?"

"Last week?"

"What day?"

She told him.

"That was the day he sent the telegram," Clint said. "How is he? He's not—"

"He's not dead, but he's in a coma."

"How badly was he shot?"

"He was hit twice, once in the shoulder and once in . . . in the head."

"The head?"

"From what I hear the doctors say it was almost a miracle. The bullet seemed to . . . skid off his skull and lodge between his head and his skull."

"And it's still there?"

"They say he's not strong enough for them to operate and remove it."

"Jesus," Clint said.

"I'm sorry, Clint. I know you're friends."

"Do you know what he was working on?"

She shook her head. "No, I don't."

"Do you know him, Ellie?"

"We've never met."

"How do you know all of this, then?"

"I heard it from Mr. Pinkerton," Ellie said. "Apparently he's been to the hospital several times since Roper was shot."

"That's interesting," Clint said. "I always suspected the old man liked Roper."

"From what I heard he likes him, but he never thought much of him as a Pinkerton," she said. "As a detective, yes, but not as a Pinkerton operative."

"Well, Tal never thought much of himself as a Pinkerton operative, either."

"He is a good detective, though."

"I don't think there was ever any argument about that," Clint said. "Tal just couldn't follow old Allan's rules."

"Few of us can," she said, wryly.

They pulled up in front of the hotel and Clint got out first, then helped Ellie down. He paid the driver and they went inside.

"What hospital is Roper in?" Clint asked her.

"St. Mary's."

Clint laughed.

"What's so funny?"

"Roper is a Catholic," Clint said, "but I don't think he's seen the inside of a church in years. When he wakes up and sees all those nuns and priests . . ."

"Can I help you, sir?" the desk clerk asked.

"Yes, I'll need a room."

"For two, sir?" the man asked, eyeing Ellie up and down.

"Just for me, friend," Clint said. "Preferably one overlooking the front."

"Yes, sir," the man said. "Please sign in, sir."

Clint signed the register and accepted his room key.

"I'm going to go upstairs and change," he said to Ellie. "Do you have anything to do today?"

"I do have something, but it shouldn't take me long," she said.

"Good, then we can have dinner."

"I'll be here at seven," she said. "What are you going to do?"

"I'm going to go to the hospital, then to Roper's office."

She kissed him, and he hugged her.

"I'm really glad to see you, Clint," she said. "If you need any help, let me know."

"I will, Ellie, thanks."

She touched his cheek and then left the hotel. Clint caught the clerk watching her and stared at him until the man cleared his throat nervously and looked away. He picked up his bag then and went up to his room.

FOUR

Clint found St. Mary's the easy way: He got into a carriage and told the driver to take him there. He noted the route so that he'd know the way next time.

He entered the hospital, which was a huge, stone structure, and stopped at the front desk. He felt slightly uncomfortable surrounded by all the religious objects—crucifixes and statues and the like. Clint Adams had never been a religious man, and when the subject of God came up, he usually found something else to talk about.

"Can I help you?" The speaker was a young nun, barely twenty if Clint was any judge—although guessing her age while she was clad in her black habit was no simple task. Still, with her fresh face and gentle eyes, she looked more like she should have been in school somewhere. Actually, she was very pretty.

"Yes, a friend of mine is here. His name is Talbot Roper."

"Oh, yes," she said, her face immediately taking a sincere look of concern and sorrow. "That poor man."

"Can I see him?"

"You will have to talk to the doctor," she said. "I'll get him for you."

"Thank you, Sister . . ."

"Ruth," she said, "my name is Sister Ruth."

He nodded, noting her name.

She started around her desk, then stopped and looked at him strangely.

"Are you a friend of Mr. Roper?" she asked then.

"Yes, Sister, I am."

"That's good," she said, reaching out and touching his right hand, which was resting on the desk. "I think he needs a friend to survive."

"Sister—"

"I'll get the doctor," she said and rushed from behind the desk.

Clint waited a few moments, and Sister Ruth returned with a tall, gaunt man who was not as old as his bald head made him appear. Clint could tell that by looking at the man's eyes.

"Mr. Adams?"

"That's right."

"I'm Doctor Frakes," the man said, extending his hand. He pronounced his name "Fra-cas." Clint accepted the hand and was impressed by the doctor's strong grip. Also, since the moment the man appeared, he had been looking directly into Clint's eyes. Clint felt that if he ever needed hospital treatment, this was the man he'd want attending to him.

"I understand you're a friend of Mr. Roper," the doctor said.

"That's right," Clint said. "I've just arrived in Denver and heard about his . . . his condition."

"He's under twenty-four-hour guard by a policeman," the doctor said, "but if you can properly identify yourself I think I can take you in to see him. It might do him some good to have a friend present."

"Well, let's go."

"No, you don't understand," the doctor said. "You will have to go to the police and identify yourself. The man in charge of Mr. Roper's case is Inspector Burns."

"Doctor, couldn't I talk to the policeman who's guarding Roper?"

"He has no authority to admit anyone," the doctor said. "I'm sorry, but this is for Mr. Roper's own protection."

"Has anyone been allowed in to see him?"

"Well, yes, as a matter of fact, Mr. Allan Pinkerton comes by from time to time. He is allowed in."

"Is that all?"

"No, Miss Russell is permitted to see him."

"Miss Russell?"

"Katherine Russell. I believe they call her Kit. She owns a restaurant of the same name. She seems to be very . . . concerned about Mr. Roper."

"I see. Anyone else?"

"Just his secretary."

"And her name?"

"Uh . . ." the doctor said, looking to Sister Ruth for help on that one.

"Her name is Carly Kirkland. She's a very nice girl."

"I'm sure she is, Sister," Doctor Frakes said. "Mr. Adams, I'm sorry I can't help you any further right now. I hope you understand."

"I do, Doctor. Can you tell me how he is?"

"The same," the doctor said. "We're waiting for his condition to improve before we try to remove the bullet."

"I see. Well, thank you, Doctor. . . . And thank *you*, Sister."

"I assume we'll be seeing you back here?" the doctor said.

"Just as soon as I can get myself properly identified, Doctor."

"I'll see him out, Doctor," Sister Ruth said.

"Uh, as you wish, Sister. I have my rounds to make."

Sister Ruth took Clint by the arm and walked him to the front door. Clint was aware that the doctor had not yet moved and was now watching them.

"I can find my way out, Sister," Clint assured her.

"I know you can," she said, tightening her hold on his arm. "Just keep walking."

He fell silent until they reached the door and stepped outside.

"What is it, Sister?"

"Your friend is in danger."

"Roper? I know that, but—"

"He does not have enough protection, Mr. Adams," Sister Ruth said. "I don't think the police are doing a good enough job of providing him with protection. Could that be because they don't like him?"

"It's possible, Sister," Clint said, wondering how much a young nun knew about 'round-the-clock protection.

"I'm not very versed in these matters, Mr. Adams," she said, as if she were reading his mind, "but I do feel that he needs better protection. Perhaps you, as his friend, can do something about it?"

"I'll certainly try, Sister," he said, "and I thank you for your concern."

"God be with you," she said, and she went back inside.

Clint went down the front steps of the hospital, thinking about what the young sister had said. He knew that Roper rebelled against authority; his experience with Allan Pinkerton made that very clear. Would the same thing happen with the police? Was Roper disliked by the Denver police, and were they not giving him full protection because of it? And what about this Inspector Burns? How did he feel about the detective?

Clint's original intention—after his conversation with Dr. Frakes—had been to go directly to the police and talk to Inspector Burns. Now he revised his plan. He was going to go and talk to Roper's secretary, Carly Kirkland, first and see what she had to say about the quality of her boss's protection.

FIVE

Clint knew where Roper's office was—or at least he thought he did. When he reached his destination, the office wasn't there anymore. In its place was an attorney's office.

"Wait for me," Clint told the carriage driver, who nodded and got comfortable.

He went to the office door and knocked, then entered. In what used to be Talbot Roper's outer office sat a woman in her fifties, not unattractive for her age, and very efficient looking.

"May I help you?" she asked.

"Yes," he said, "I *was* looking for Talbot Roper's office."

"The detective?"

"Yes."

"I'm afraid he moved a couple of months ago, and we took over these offices."

"Would you know where he moved to?"

"As a matter of fact I do. He left us the address so we could forward mail. I have some here. I've already written his new address on it, and I was going to put it in the mail today."

"I can take it to him."

She thought a moment, then said, "All right." She opened a drawer, took out a few envelopes, and handed them to him.

Clint looked at the address she had written on the envelopes and was surprised that Talbot Roper had moved his business to a much less desirable part of town.

"Thank you, ma'am. I'll see that he gets these."

"Excuse me," she said as he started to leave.

"Yes?"

"I read where Mr. Roper had been shot. Is he going to be all right?"

"It's a little too soon to tell that, ma'am."

"I see. Well, I hope he *is* all right."

"I'll pass along your concern, ma'am." Clint tipped his hat and said, "Good day to you."

He went outside and showed the address to the half-asleep driver.

"I know where that is," he said. "You don't want to go there, do you?"

"I do."

"It'll cost you extra."

"What for?"

"Hazard pay."

Clint eyed the man and saw that he was dead serious.

"All right, let's go. You'll get your hazard pay."

When the man walked into the office Carly Kirkland looked up from her desk nervously. They had been in this location for two months now, and she still wasn't used to it. Since Roper's shooting she walked the streets in this area with even more trepidation than usual.

"Miss Kirkland?" the man asked.

"That's right," she said. "Mr. Roper's not here, so if you've come about hiring—"

"My name is Clint Adams, Miss Kirkland," the man said, interrupting her. "I'm a friend of Roper's."

"Adams?" she said, frowning.

"Maybe this will explain it better," he said, handing her a telegram.

While Carly Kirkland read the telegram, Clint looked

around the office. There were two desks sharing the room, the other apparently belonging to Roper. Clint wondered why Roper had moved here.

"I remember now," she said. "He sent this the day . . . the day he was shot."

She started to cry then, and Clint stopped looking at the office and looked at the girl.

She appeared to be in her early twenties, perhaps not much older than Sister Ruth. She was not pretty, but she had an interesting face. Her nose was a little too big, but she did have pretty eyes and silky black hair. The last time Clint had seen Roper in Denver he had been between secretaries. Girls were as transient with Roper as they were with Rick Hartman in Labyrinth.

"How long have you worked for Roper?" he asked.

"Three months."

"When did you move the office here?"

"Two months ago."

"Why?"

She dabbed at her nose with a tissue, then discarded it.

"Mr. Roper could no longer afford the rent on his other offices."

"Couldn't afford the rent?" Clint asked. "Has the business fallen on hard times?"

"I'm afraid you will have to ask Mr. Roper about his business," she said. "I only know what he told me."

Clint studied the girl's face for a few moments, then said, "Oh, I'll bet you know more than that, a smart girl like you."

"And what makes you think I'm smart?"

"You look smart and you sound smart," Clint said. "Are you going to tell me you're not?"

She smiled then and said, "No, I'm not going to tell you that. No, business has not been so good. His former secretary quit because he wanted to cut her salary. I, on the other hand, found his offer more than I could get working elsewhere . . . since I didn't have prior experience."

"You looked a little nervous when I walked in," he remarked.

"In this area, you never know *who* is going to walk in," she said.

"It must be hard for you to come to work here without him around."

"It's . . . starting to affect my nerves," she admitted.

"Could your nerves stand a little lunch?"

"I *am* hungry," she said, biting her lower lip. "I didn't bring anything with me today, and I was hesitant to go out and get something."

"Come on," he said, "I'll buy you lunch and keep you safe at the same time."

"That's a very generous offer," she said, "and I'm too hungry to even think about turning it down."

"I hope you won't mind answering a few questions while we eat?"

"If it's the price I have to pay to eat," she said, "I'll answer them as best I can."

"Can't ask more than that," he said.

SIX

Clint paid off the carriage driver and then walked Carly Kirkland out of the area so they could eat in a decent restaurant. They passed two young men a couple of doors down from the office, both of whom gave Carly wide, leering smiles and tipped their hats.

"Friends of yours?" Clint asked.

"Hardly," she said. "They've been making remarks to me since the day we moved here. Luckily, they don't seem inclined to do anything more."

"If you don't mind me saying so," he said, "you appear capable of handling yourself around here."

"When I'm outside I strive to make it look that way," she said. "When I'm inside I give in to my nerves, for want of a better way."

"There is no better way, Miss Kirkland."

When they were seated in a small restaurant in a better neighborhood, Carly Kirkland leaned forward and said, "Since you're a friend of Mr. Roper, and since you're buying me lunch, I suppose you had better call me 'Carly.' "

"All right," he said, "and I suppose you had better call me 'Clint.' "

"I warn you," she said, picking up the menu, "I eat like a horse when I'm this hungry."

"Order whatever you like, Carly."

She grinned across the table at him and said, "You must have a lot of questions."

"Only a few, actually," he said. "They can wait until after we order."

They *did* order, and Carly was more than right. She ordered more food than Clint did and seemed quite capable of eating every bit of it.

"We can talk while we eat," Carly said.

"Tell me about Roper's relationship with Inspector Burns."

"They don't have one," she said.

"Do they like each other?"

"Oh, I see what you mean," she said. "No, Inspector Burns doesn't like Mr. Roper. I can't think of a policeman who does."

"What about you?"

"What about me?"

"Do you like him?"

"Sure," she said. "He's a good boss."

"Is he a good man?"

"From what I can see," she said, "and I only see him during working hours."

"Can you understand why the police wouldn't like him?" he asked.

"Oh, I think so," she said. "He gets a lot of newspaper coverage when he works on a case—at least he used to."

"When did things go wrong?" he asked. "And how?"

"I really can't answer that," she said. "Things had gone wrong, as you say, before he hired me."

"All right," he said. "Have you been to the hospital?"

"Of course."

"What do you think of the protection they're giving him there?"

"I don't think much of it," she said. "I tried to tell Inspector Burns that, but he chewed my head off. He told me to mind my business."

"They have one man watching him at a time?"

"Yes, and I've never seen a man who looked particularly

efficient. A couple of them looked so old they couldn't have stopped me from entering the room—if I didn't already have permission, that is. Did they let you see him?''

''No, they said I had to see Burns first, but I wanted to talk to you before I did that. There's a young nun there who feels the same way you do.''

''That would be Sister Ruth,'' Carly said. ''We've become friends since . . . since Mr. Roper was shot.''

''Carly, do you know what Roper was working on when he was shot?''

She stopped eating to answer that one.

''He didn't really confide in me, Clint. I'm mostly a paper shuffler, keeping files straight, sending out bills and overdue notices—when there are overdue notices to send out.''

''Carly, are you sure you can't tell me why a successful detective practice suddenly went sour?'' Clint asked her again.

''I'm sorry, Clint,'' she said, shaking her head, ''but I just don't know.''

''Well,'' he said, fiddling with his fork, ''I might be able to figure out what he was working on if I can have a look at his desk.''

''Do you think that would tell you who shot him?'' she asked.

''It might,'' he said. ''Of course, I can't look at his desk without your okay.''

''You're being nice,'' she said. ''You could look at it if you wanted to.''

''I'd rather you let me in to do it.''

''Well, finish your lunch then, and we'll go back and look at it right away.''

''Together?''

''Yes, together,'' she said. ''I've been working for him for three months and I'm tired of shuffling paper. I think it's time I got a little more involved, don't you?''

''Oh, definitely, Carly,'' Clint said. ''Absolutely.''

SEVEN

After lunch they walked back to the office, passing the same two young men who made kissing noises at Carly. Clint stopped and was going to approach them when Carly pulled on his arm.

"Believe me, Clint," she said, "they're not worth your time."

"They should learn something about respect."

"If it doesn't bother me it shouldn't bother you."

She had a point there.

She let them in with her key and locked the door behind them.

"All right," she said, "there's his desk. See what it can tell you."

"*Us,*" he reminded her, "let's see what it can tell *us*."

She smiled, her face brightening, and she said, "All right!"

She joined Clint by the desk and started opening drawers, then she stopped and looked at him.

"What are we looking for?"

"Current cases," Clint said. "Would you have filed them yet?"

"It depends," she said. "If they were closed—but then, he didn't have many cases these last couple of months."

"And he didn't talk to you about the ones he had?"

"No."

"All right," Clint said. "If he's working on something

now, let's assume it's either in or on the desk."
"Then I'll take in," she said.
"And I'll take on," Clint said.

They went through the desk for an hour and along the way switched responsibilities. Clint took the inside and Carly took the top, and they still couldn't find anything that would tell them something.
"You know what?" Clint said.
"What?"
"It's in his head."
"What is?"
"The case, whatever he's been working on or whatever he was about to work on. It's not down on paper, it's in his head."
"But . . . he can't tell us anything."
"He will," Clint said, "when he comes around."
"What if he doesn't?" she asked. "What if he dies?"
"He's too ornery to die."
"But what if—"
"Carly," Clint said, cutting her off, "if he were to tell someone, if he *wanted* to tell someone what he was working on, who would it be?"
"That's easy," she said. "Kit Russell."
"The doctor at the hospital mentioned her. She owns a restaurant?"
"Yes."
"Do you know where it is?"
"Any driver in the city knows where it is," she said. "Just grab a carriage and tell him you want to go there."
"All right, I'll do that. How close were they?"
"I don't know."
"More than just friends?"
"I don't know, Clint," she said. "Mr. Roper talked to me even less about his personal life."
"All right," Clint said, "I'll have to ask her."

He started for the door, then stopped.

"Carly, let me give you a ride home."

She stared at him for a moment, then said, "I can't. We made a mess and I have to clean it up."

"Go home, Carly," he said. "I'll come back tomorrow and help you straighten up."

She thought a moment, then said, "Promise?"

He smiled at her and said, "Yes, I promise."

Clint hailed a carriage and Carly gave the driver her address. When they reached her building he told the driver to wait.

"I'll walk you up," he said.

"All right."

She opened the front door with her key and led him to the second floor, to the door of her apartment.

"I'll come by here and pick you up tomorrow, then we'll go to the office and clean up," Clint said.

"We can meet there," she said.

"No, I'll pick you up."

She put her key in the lock and then turned to him and said, "You don't have to keep your promise, you know."

He smiled at her and kissed her on the cheek.

"I always keep my promises, Carly. I'll see you tomorrow."

She touched her cheek, then opened the door and went inside.

As he turned away, her door opened and she said, "Oh, by the way."

"What?"

"The restaurant? It's called Kit's."

"Kit's," he repeated.

"Just tell the driver."

"See you tomorrow."

She closed her door, and he went downstairs to the waiting carriage.

"You know a place called Kit's?" he asked the driver.

"I sure do."

"Take me there."

"I'll take you to your hotel first."

"Why?"

The driver gave Clint a pointed look and said, "You're gonna want to change your clothes."

EIGHT

When Clint Adams arrived at Kit's Place he understood why the carriage driver had suggested a change of clothes. He was wearing the best suit he had—he always packed it when he went to Denver or San Francisco—and he still felt grossly underdressed.

He paid off the driver, giving him a big tip for his help, and went to the front door of the place. There he was met by the largest doorman he'd ever seen.

"Can I help you?" the man asked.

"Uh, no, I'd just like to go inside."

"Do you have a reservation?"

"No," Clint said, "I didn't know I needed one."

"Are you alone?"

Clint looked around and said, "I seem to be."

With patience the big man said, "Are you meeting anyone?"

"No," Clint said, sorry he'd made fun of the man.

"Well, you might be able to get a small table," the man started, but Clint interrupted him.

"I don't want a table."

"You don't? Are you interested in something else?"

The driver had told Clint that there were sometimes "games of chance" held on the premises, so he understood what the man meant.

"No, nothing else," Clint said. "I would like to see Miss Katherine Russell."

Now the man frowned and looked Clint Adams up and down carefully. Clint had left his big Colt home and had the little Colt New Line in his pocket.

"Do you have an appointment?"

"No, I don't," Clint said, and it was his turn to exhibit some patience. He never expected to have this much difficulty just getting into a restaurant.

"I'm afraid Miss Russell doesn't see anyone without an appointment."

"Maybe if we ask her, she'll see me."

"That's possible," the man said, but he didn't make a move to do so.

"Can we ask her?"

"Perhaps at another time, sir," the man said, "when we are not so busy."

"Are you always this busy?"

"Yes."

"Then maybe it had better be tonight."

There was some steel in Clint's tone, and the big man reacted to it, straightening his back.

"Sir—"

"Tell her it's about Talbot Roper."

"Mr. Roper?" the man said. "Are you . . . a friend of his?"

"I am."

The big man looked as if he were trying to make a decision.

"What is your name, sir?"

"Adams," Clint said, "Clint Adams."

"Wait here."

He watched as the man opened the door, leaned inside, and spoke to someone out of sight. He never once moved his huge frame enough for Clint to get by.

"Well?" Clint asked as the big man's head reappeared.

"It will be a moment, sir."

Clint stepped aside as a man and woman approached.

The man spoke his name to the doorman, who admitted him with no problem.

"I guess he had a reservation, huh?" Clint said.

The big man gave him a stony stare and did not bother answering.

It took about five minutes rather than a moment, but the door finally opened from the inside and someone said something to the doorman.

"You can go inside, sir," the doorman said to Clint. "There's someone inside who will take you to see Miss Russell."

"Thank you," Clint said.

The man moved aside and Clint opened the door, entered, and found himself face to face with—the same man? No, it wasn't the same man. This one was dressed a little differently, which is the only way Clint *knew* that it wasn't the same man. Other than the clothes, he was the exact duplicate of the man on the outside.

"Brothers?" Clint asked.

"Follow me, sir," the second big man said.

Clint shrugged and followed the big man through another door and into the restaurant.

If he was impressed on the outside, Clint was even more impressed on the inside. Everything was leather and stained glass, and it all gleamed as if it had just been shined.

He followed the big man, skirting the tables so that they never got in the way of the waiters or the diners. They went to a stairway in the back of the room and up to a hallway. There was a wooden rail that looked freshly waxed, and when Clint looked down he could see the entire room below.

"This way," the big man said, as Clint had paused a moment. He noticed that this brother—and it was obvious that they *were* brothers, even though no one had confirmed it—was not as polite as the doorman. Maybe that was why the other brother had the outside job. If *he* was the doorman, *this* one had to be the bouncer.

"Lead on," Clint said.

He followed the man to a curtained doorway—an expensive, red brocade curtain—into a smaller hallway and to a shining oak door. The big man knocked, opened the door, and waved Clint in.

"Thank you for the tour," Clint said, passing him and entering the room.

Knowing Talbot Roper as he did, and knowing how the man loved beautiful women, Clint should have been prepared for the woman who stood behind the huge oak desk, but he was not.

No one could have been fully prepared for a woman like this.

She was tall and full breasted, with skin like milk and hair like fire, which was worn piled high on her head. Any normal man would wonder what that hair would look like cascading down her back and over her shoulders—which was exactly what Clint was wondering.

The blue evening gown she wore was cut just low enough to show the beginnings of her full cleavage. This was not a woman who needed to show herself off. She knew people would be looking at her regardless.

As Clint Adams was now.

NINE

"I understand you're a friend of Talbot Roper," she said.

"Nice to meet you too," he said.

Her jaw tightened, and he closed some of the distance between them. His guess was that she was probably in her midtwenties. He didn't let the lines around her eyes and at the corners of her mouth throw him. Her eyes were somewhat bleary, and he felt that she had probably been under a great strain of late.

It probably had something to do with Roper.

"Let's start again," she said. "I'm Katherine Russell."

"Clint Adams, Miss Russell," he said. She extended her hand and he took it, sure that he was not getting her best handshake.

"I'm sorry—" he started, but she waved away his protest.

"I'm tired, and I'm losing my manners," she said. Suddenly she wavered a bit, and he was around the desk and at her side. She sagged against him.

"I'm sorry," she said, "I'm just very . . . tired. . . ."

"You'd better sit down before you fall down," he said, easing her into her chair.

"Thank you."

He regretted that her body was no longer leaning against him, and he hastily took his hands from her shoulders. She was, after all—*probably*—Talbot Roper's woman.

"Is there some brandy around?" he asked.

"In that cabinet," she said, waving her hand to her left.

He saw an oak cabinet—*everything* here that was wood was oak, of that he was now sure—and walked to it. He opened the double doors and found a small but well-stocked bar. He located the brandy and poured her some.

"Thank you," she said as he handed her the glass. She sipped it and said, "I'm all right now. Pour yourself something and please sit."

"I'll just sit," he said.

"Roper's mentioned you from time to time," she said, putting the glass down on the desk. Roper's last name sounded odd coming from her mouth. He thought he knew why.

"Tal crosses my mind from time to time as well," he said. He felt she'd been waiting for *him* to use the familiar form of Roper's name—"Tal," which was what his friends called him.

"Yes," she said, forcing a smile, "he crosses mine from time to time as well."

"Moreso of late?" he asked.

"Yes," she said wearily.

"Miss Russell, I can't prove who I am—not right at this minute—but I would like to talk to you about Talbot Roper and what's happened to him. Wait—" he said then, remembering the telegram Roper had sent him. He had it in his pocket. He took it out and gave it to her.

She read it, then handed it back.

"Of course," he said, putting it back into his pocket, "this doesn't prove who I am."

"You needn't prove anything, Mr. Adams. Just tell me what I can do."

"Well, I'd like to try and find out two things. One is, of course, who shot Tal, but the police might be better suited to that job than I am."

"I doubt that," she said sourly, "but go ahead. What's the second thing?"

"I'd like to find out why he sent for me," Clint said.

"I can't help you," she said. "I hadn't . . . seen him for several days before he was shot, and then . . . that same night . . ." She broke off, touching two fingers to her forehead.

"What happened that night?" he asked.

"We had . . . an argument," she said. He knew she was fighting tears, and he gave her the few moments she needed.

"At least *I* was trying to have an argument," she said. "I was angry—miffed, actually—at not having seen him. He said he was working on something, but I . . . I still gave him a hard time." She stopped as the tears threatened to make their appearance again, then said through them, "If he dies that's the last thing he'll remember about me."

"He's not going to die," Clint said.

"How can you be sure?"

"This telegram says something about a lot of money," Clint said. "If there's a lot of money to be had somehow, Talbot Roper is not going to let a little thing like getting shot stand in his way."

She smiled then, if somewhat wanly, and said, "You know him that well. You really are the Gunsmith."

He winced but did not take her to task for using the name.

"Miss Russell—"

"Please," she said, pulling a tissue out of a drawer, "call me 'Kit.'"

"All right," he said, "and you call me 'Clint.' Kit, if I could find out what he was working on it would go a long way toward telling me why he sent for me."

"I'm sorry," she said, "but I can't help you. He didn't talk about business with me."

"Can you tell me what went wrong with his business?"

"Wrong?"

"Why he had to move his office, why he hadn't been getting many cases recently."

She frowned.

"I knew nothing about that," she said, looking puzzled. "He moved his office."

"Yes, to a much less desirable—and less expensive—part of the city."

She sat up straighter and asked, "Was that why he hadn't been coming around so much? He was having problems?"

"It looks like he was having some definite money problems, as well as trouble finding work."

"But that's absurd," she said. "He's the best at what he does. Even that old buzzard Allan Pinkerton knows that. What could have gone wrong?"

It was obvious that she knew nothing about Roper's recent difficulties.

"Whatever it is," Clint said, "I guess he didn't want his friends to know."

"He could have come to me if he needed money—"

"I'm sure he knew that," Clint said, interrupting her, "but you know as well as I do that he'd never do that."

"I know," she said, "I know."

"Well," he said, "if you can't help me I guess I'll be going."

"Where?" she asked.

He stood up. "I have to talk to the police. It seems I need their clearance to see Tal."

"That means you'll have to talk to Inspector Burns," she said, pronouncing the man's name with obvious distaste.

"I take it you don't think much of the inspector?"

"I try to think about him as little as possible."

"Then what I've heard about his relationship with Tal must be true."

"He *hated* Tal!" she said vehemently. "He's probably the happiest man in Denver right now, and the only thing that could make him happier would be for Talbot Roper to die!"

"Well, I'll have to get his okay to see Tal," Clint said. "I have no choice but to talk to him."

"Tell him you're working for me."

"What?"

"Tell him I hired you to find out what happened to Tal," she said.

"I'm not a detective," Clint argued.

"I know that," she said, "but I have a certain . . . position in Denver, and anything you have to do will be easier if you say you're working for me—especially with Burns. He may be a . . . he has a healthy respect for people of position."

"All right," Clint said. "I'll hold that as an ace in the hole, if I need it."

"*Any* time you need it," she said.

"Thank you."

"Where will you be dining tonight?" she asked as he moved toward the door.

"I hadn't thought about it."

"Please eat here," she said. "I'll have a table held for you. I'd like to know how your meeting with the inspector goes."

"All right," he said. "Thanks."

"Clint?"

"Yes."

"How long will you be here?"

"Until I find out what's going on," he said.

"Good," she said, and he was pleased that she looked visibly relieved.

When he reached the door, she called out, "He won't know you're there, you know."

"What?"

"Tal," she said, sadly, "when you go to see him, he won't know you're there."

He smiled at her and said, "Maybe he will."

TEN

Clint entered the police station and walked up to the uniformed policeman behind the desk.

"Can I help you?" the policeman asked.

"I'd like to see Inspector Burns."

"You would?" the man asked, looking surprised. He was in his late forties, with slate-gray hair, and had probably been a policeman for a long time. He had that tired look all old lawmen get.

"Yes, I would."

The man shrugged, as if to say it was up to Clint if he wanted to put himself through that.

"Have a seat and I'll tell him," the man said. "What's it about?"

"It's about the shooting of Talbot Roper."

"Oh, that," the man said. "That's his favorite subject these days. Have a seat."

There was a long wooden bench nearby and Clint sat down on it, while the older policeman sent a younger one to tell Burns he had a visitor.

After a few moments a man came down a flight of stairs and walked over to the desk.

"Who wants to see me, Sam?"

"Over there, Jack," the desk policeman said, indicating Clint with a careless wave of his hand.

Inspector Jack Burns turned around and looked at Clint Adams.

Burns was an ugly man. There was just no other, kinder way to put it. He was probably the ugliest man Clint had ever seen. His nose was too small for his face, and beneath it his lips were too big. His eyebrows were bushy black and his eyes small and mean. He had black hair, but it was thinning up on top, and he probably held that against the world. His age was hard to gauge, but Clint guessed he was probably fifty.

"What can I do for you?" he asked Clint from across the room.

Clint rose and walked up to the man, who was even uglier up close.

"My name is Clint Adams, Inspector," Clint said. "I understand you're the man I have to see to get in to visit Talbot Roper."

"I am," Burns said. "Why do you want to see him?"

"He's a friend of mine."

"He ain't awake."

"I'd like to see him anyway."

"He may never wake up," Burns said, but it was as if he were talking to himself, reminding himself of something very good that had happened recently.

"That may be so, but I'd like to ask some questions about what happened, and I'd like to get your . . . permission to see him."

"Well, I don't care if you go in and see him," Burns said, "but why should I answer any questions?"

"It's not that I don't think you're doing your best to find out who shot him," Clint said, choosing his words very carefully, "but I'd like to ask around myself and see what I can do to help."

"Are you some kind of lawman?"

"No."

"A detective?"

"Not exactly."

"What does that mean, 'not exactly'?"

Clint decided to go ahead and use Kit's name and see what that got him.

"I've been asked by Miss Katherine Russell to look into the incident."

"Russell?" Burns said, his face falling. "Is that *Kit* Russell?"

"I believe she's called that, yes," Clint said. "She assured me that I'd have your cooperation."

"Well," Burns said, grudgingly, "if you're working for Miss Russell . . ."

"You can check with her, if you like."

"Don't worry," Burns said, "I will. Come back to my office with me and I'll try and answer your questions."

"Thank you, Inspector."

Clint spent about twenty minutes with Burns, which for him was twenty minutes too much. The man answered questions grudgingly and showed absolutely no enthusiasm for finding whoever had shot Talbot Roper.

"Let me be honest with you, Adams," Burns said. "Roper and I weren't exactly buddies, and I can't say I'm sorry he was shot, but that don't mean I'm not trying to find out who did it."

Sure, Clint thought, you're just not trying all that hard!

"So you don't know what cases he was working on when he was shot?"

"No," Burns said, "and that secretary of his is a waste. She's as dumb as a stone."

Obviously, Burns didn't take the time to really talk with Carly or he would have known that wasn't true.

"So you're not anywhere near finding out who killed him?"

"No," Inspector Burns said, without the slightest hint of regret.

"What about witnesses?"

"None."

"How many people do you have working on it?"

"Just me."

"That's all?"

Burns smirked and said, "If I can't find the shooter, nobody can."

That remains to be seen, Clint thought.

"All right, Inspector," Clint said, standing up, "if you'll just give me something I can show to the man guarding Roper's room so that he'll let me in, I'll be on my way."

"Sure," Burns said. He pulled a piece of paper out of his desk and wrote something down, then signed it. He passed it over to Clint. "You be sure to tell Miss Russell I cooperated."

"Oh, I will," Clint said, accepting the pass. "Oh, by the way."

"Yeah?"

"How many men are watching the hospital?"

"Just one—the man on the door."

"Do you think that's enough?"

Burns smirked again and said, "It's plenty."

"Aren't you afraid the shooter might come back and try to finish the job?"

"I don't have any more men to put in the hospital, Adams," Burns said. "We can't have men just sitting around all day doing nothing."

"I see," Clint said. He folded up the pass and put it in his pocket. "Thanks for all your . . . help, Inspector Burns."

"Yeah, you're welcome. You're not from Denver, are you?"

"No, I'm not."

"I don't know what Miss Russell thinks you can do that I can't," Burns said.

Clint was at the door, and he turned to look at Burns before leaving.

"Maybe she thinks I can care."

ELEVEN

From the police station Clint went back to the hospital. As he had hoped, Sister Ruth was still on duty at the desk.

"Hello, Sister," he said.

Her head had been bent over her work, and when she looked up and saw him, she smiled.

"Hello, welcome back. Did you have any trouble?"

"No," Clint said. "I have a pass. Can you tell me where Roper's room is?"

"I'll take you there," she said, coming around the desk. She took hold of his elbow and said, "Come."

They walked down the halls together, turning right and then left, and finally Clint saw a uniformed policeman sitting in front of a door. The man was white-haired and had to be in his sixties. At the moment he was sitting with his chair tilted back, sound asleep.

"I see what you meant, Sister."

"It's a disgrace."

Clint approached the room and the sleeping man and pushed the door open. The man didn't stir, so Clint didn't bother to wake him. He just shrugged at Sister Ruth and went inside.

The room was dark, and in the center of it was a bed. Clint moved closer and was able to make out the features of Talbot Roper. The detective looked drawn and pale, and for a moment Clint thought he might have stopped breathing, but as he continued to stare he saw the man's chest rising and falling evenly.

"I got your message, Tal," Clint said. "Now, how about waking up and telling me what it's all about?"

He waited a few moments, but there was no sign that the man had heard him.

Clint opened his mouth to speak again, then closed it, feeling foolish talking to someone who couldn't hear a word he said. He looked around the room and saw that there was only one window. He walked to it and saw that it wasn't even locked, so he locked it. It wasn't much of a lock, though, and it certainly wouldn't keep anyone out who really wanted to enter.

Satisfied that Roper was alive, he turned and left the room. The policeman slept on, and Clint went to join Sister Ruth again, who had waited for him.

"Why didn't you wake him?" she asked.

"He looks like he could use the rest."

"But your friend—"

"I'm going to see if I can have some people of my own come and look after him, Sister."

"That would probably be wise."

"Would you show them around the hospital?"

"I'd be glad to."

"They'll want to see all the entrances and exits."

"I'll do whatever I can to help, Mr. Adams."

"Clint," he said, "my name is Clint."

"All right, Clint," Sister Ruth said.

When they reached the front door she asked, "How many people will you be sending?"

"I don't know," Clint said. "I'm not sure yet, Sister."

"But you will be sending someone, won't you?"

"I hope so," Clint said. "If I can't get anyone, I'll just have to come and sit here myself."

"That would be fine with me," Sister Ruth said. "I could use the company."

"I'll see you soon, Sister."

"Go with God."

As he walked down the steps, he was thinking about what she had said *before* "Go with God."

Was it his imagination, or had a nun just flirted with him?

TWELVE

"We're eating where?" Ellie asked.

They were in Clint's room, where Ellie had come to pick him up for dinner.

"At Kit's Place."

"Have you ever been to Kit's Place?" she asked.

"Uh, yes, I have, today."

"I've *never* been there," she said. "I haven't ever been able to afford it."

"What about the men who take you to dinner?"

"They can't afford it either. Why did you pick that place?"

"Come on," Clint said, opening the door, "I'll tell you on the way."

In the carriage Clint told Ellie about Talbot Roper and Kit Russell.

"So Kit Russell is in love with Roper?"

"I'd say so."

"And what about him?"

He shrugged. "That I can't tell you, Ellie," he said. "I know Roper likes women—"

"Like somebody else we know?" she asked.

He ignored the remark and just said, "I just don't know if he'd ever commit himself to one woman."

"Well, I guess nobody knows that but him."

"I have something else I'd like to talk to you about," he said, "but we'll discuss that at the restaurant."

"I wish you'd told me sooner where we were going," she grumbled. "I'd have dressed better."

"You look fine," he said, and she did look lovely in a simple green dress.

The carriage pulled up in front of the restaurant and Clint helped Ellie down. When they approached the front door, Ellie saw the huge doorman.

"I've heard stories about him," she said, doubtfully.

"What kind of stories?"

"He's impossible to get past if you don't know the right people."

"Well, let's see if I do."

As they reached the entrance, the doorman opened the door and said, "Nice to see you again, Mr. Adams."

"Thank you . . ."

"Dutch" the man said. "My name is Dutch."

"Thank you, Dutch."

"I hope you and your lovely companion enjoy dinner."

"We will," Ellie said.

As they entered, she took hold of Clint's arm and squeezed it. "This is exciting! I *never* thought I'd ever come here, and I certainly never expected to be treated like . . . like *that*!"

The maitre d' approached them. "Excuse me, sir? Will there be more than two in your party?" Clint was relieved to see that the man was not related to Maurice the doorman or his brother. He was about five-ten, slender, dark haired and dark skinned, and was somewhere in his thirties.

"No," Clint said, "just the two of us."

"And your name?"

"Adams," Clint said, "Clint Adams."

"Oh yes, of course," the man said, "Mr. Adams. Please follow me. Your table is waiting."

"Thank you."

Clint and Ellie followed the man to what was obviously a table for four, which had been set for two.

"Is this table all right, sir?"

"It's fine," Clint said.

The man held Ellie's chair for her and when Clint was seated said, "My name is Christopher, sir. If you need anything, please don't hesitate to call. Your waiter's name is Henry. He will be right with you."

"That's fine."

While waiting for the waiter, Ellie tried to quell her excitement by getting back to business. "What was it you wanted to talk to me about?"

"I was at the hospital today," he said.

"You saw Roper?"

"Yes."

"How is he?"

"The same," he said. "He wasn't conscious when I was there, but I went there more to take a look at how he was being protected."

"And was he?"

"Yes, by a sleeping sixty-year-old policeman."

"Oh."

"That's what I want to talk to you about," Clint said. "I want to put some people in the hospital."

"Some people?"

"Private people."

"Well, I'd be glad to help."

"What about Pinkerton?"

"What about him?"

"Do you think *he'd* help?"

"Sure," she said, "if you paid him."

"I could talk to him."

"You and he never seem to be able to just *talk*."

"We just don't see eye to eye."

After a moment she said, "*I* could talk to him."

"Would you?"

"What do you need?"

"Just a couple of men," he said, and when she glared at him he added, "or women."

"For free?"

"He's been to the hospital, Ellie," he said. "He must have *some* feelings for Roper."

"He has respect for Roper," she said, "but that doesn't mean he's going to commit some of his people for *free*."

"Well, if he doesn't I'll just have to get them from somewhere else."

"Well, I have some vacation time coming, so you can count on me."

"Thanks, Ellie."

The waiter came then, with menus, and had a discussion with them about what to order. Apparently Kit Russell had instructed that Clint be given the red-carpet treatment, and her employees were following her instructions to the letter.

They ordered according to the waiter's suggestions and were not disappointed. The food was excellent, as was the wine. (Clint had almost ordered beer but decided against it. It just didn't go with the ambience.)

After the dinner plates had been cleared away Henry, the waiter, came back and asked if they would be interested in coffee and dessert.

"I'll have coffee," Clint said.

"How do you like it, sir?"

"Black and strong."

"Of course. And the lady?"

"I'll have a cup of tea and something with a lot of chocolate."

"I have just the thing," Henry said with a smile, and he went off to get it.

While they were waiting for dessert to be served, Clint saw Kit Russell crossing the dining room to them. She was acknowledging the greetings of people along the way, but her eyes were on Clint. She was wearing a different gown—

a stunning red one with a plunging neckline that showed her full breasts off to great advantage.

"Here comes the owner," he said.

Ellie turned her head, and Clint saw her eyes widen when she saw Kit Russell.

"That's Kit Russell?"

"That's her."

"She's stunning!"

Seldom had Clint heard such admiration for one woman coming from another.

"Yes, she is," he agreed.

When she reached the table, he stood up.

"I'm glad you accepted my invitation," Kit said, extending her hand.

Clint shook the proffered hand and said, "It was worth it."

Kit turned to Ellie and asked, "Did you enjoy the meal?"

"Oh, yes, it was wonderful."

"I'm glad."

"You have a lovely place here, Miss Russell."

"Please, call me 'Kit.' "

"I'm sorry," Clint said. "Kit Russell, meet Ellie Lennox."

The two women exchanged greetings, and when Ellie asked Kit to sit with them she accepted.

"Ellie is a Pinkerton operative," Clint said, thinking that Kit might be curious about his partner.

"Really? That's fascinating," Kit said. She looked at Ellie and said, "I didn't think there *were* any female detectives. How exciting it must be for you!"

"Sometimes, yes," Ellie said. "Unfortunately, Mr. Pinkerton is not quite ready to let women work on the same assignments as men."

"I'm sure you'll show him the error of his ways, Ellie," Kit said. She looked at Clint then and asked, "Did you do everything you wanted to do today?"

"Yes, I did," he said. He told her about the visit to Inspector Burns and then about the hospital.

"I'm hoping to get some private people to keep an eye on the hospital and on Tal. Ellie is willing to help, and I'm going to ask Pinkerton for some help, though I doubt he'll do it for nothing."

"I'll pay," Kit said.

"I'm sorry," Clint said quickly, "I didn't mean to imply you should—"

"I know you didn't, but I don't know why I didn't think of it sooner," Kit said, cutting him off. "Inspector Burns obviously isn't going to take the best care of Tal. That means it's up to us, his friends."

"I wish I had some people I knew," Clint said. "I know Pinkerton has reliable men, but they probably don't like Tal any more than Inspector Burns does."

"I could supply you with some people," Kit said, "but they wouldn't be detectives."

"I don't necessarily want detectives," Clint said. "I want people with sharp eyes who wouldn't be afraid if things got rough."

"I know just the ones," Kit said. "I'll talk to them, of course, and see if they're willing to help, but I think they will be. Everyone here likes Tal."

Clint wondered if she were going to ask the twins if they'd be interested. He wasn't sure how he'd feel looking at the same face twice all the time. It might affect his eyes.

"Well, I think I'll watch the hospital tonight," Clint said, "and then maybe we could meet tomorrow to see who you've come up with."

"That will be fine," Kit said, "but should you be doing this alone, tonight?"

"Oh, he won't be doing it alone," Ellie said quickly.

Kit looked at Ellie and smiled. "No, I can see that he won't."

At that point Henry came with dessert, and Kit stood up.

"I'll leave you to your dessert." She started to turn away, then said, "Oh, by the way."

"What?" Clint asked.

"Did you have to use my name with Inspector Burns?"

"Oh, yeah," Clint said, "and he became *very* cooperative. Thanks."

"I'm glad it worked," she said. She looked at Ellie and said, "I'm very glad to have met you, Ellie. I hope we'll be seeing each other again."

"I'm sure we will," Ellie said. "Thank you."

Kit looked at Clint and said, "Of course, there will be no check," and she walked away before he could object.

"She's wonderful," Ellie said.

Clint was reserving his opinion.

"Yes," Henry said, "she is."

They both looked up at the portly, balding waiter, who seemed to have embarrassed himself. The man cleared his throat and served them dessert.

THIRTEEN

From Kit's Place they went back to Clint's hotel room and went to bed.

It was months since they'd seen each other and their lovemaking reflected that.

The first time was very quick, both of them eager to get reacquainted with each other.

The second time Clint deliberately slowed the pace, and Ellie did not object, especially not when he got down between her legs and began to lick her, tasting her with slow, easy, lapping motions of his tongue, teasing her until she moaned aloud and reached for his head. He found her clit then and flicked at it with his tongue until she lifted her buttocks off the bed, her body as taut as a bowstring as she was on the verge of orgasm.

Before that orgasm had faded he was inside of her, cupping her buttocks in his hands and pulling her tightly to him. She reached around to squeeze his buttocks while he took her in long, slow strokes, and this time they both came together. . . .

"Why don't you think they've tried for him again before now?" she asked later.

They were lying together, resting. Clint had decided that they would not go to the hospital until midnight, and he wondered if Sister Ruth would still be there then.

"I don't know," Clint said. "Maybe his wounds were

serious enough that they expected him to die. If that's the case, they must be getting tired of waiting. I know I would be."

"You didn't find out anything at his office?"

"No," Clint said. "His secretary's only been with him a couple of months, and he doesn't talk to her about cases."

"What about his files?"

"Lots of old cases but not many new ones."

"I'd heard some rumblings about his falling on hard times."

"I wonder what caused it," he asked, more to himself than to her.

"It happens to people, Clint," she said. "Sometimes your luck runs out."

"Talbot Roper has always been good at making his own luck."

"Well, this time it doesn't look good," she said. "If he's got some magic up his sleeve, he'd better pull it out and use it soon."

Clint agreed.

Clint woke at eleven and shook Ellie awake.

"I'm up," she said sleepily.

As they began dressing, Clint said, "You know I appreciate you doing this with me, but don't you have to be at work tomorrow?"

"I'll just send word that I'm under the weather," she said. "Since we're staying awake all night, by morning that should be more than true."

When they were dressed, Clint debated whether or not to wear his gunbelt. He decided not to, but he would take the big Colt with him and he tucked it into his belt.

"Do you have a gun?"

"Yes," she said, "in my bag."

"All right, let's go then."

They went downstairs and Clint asked the hotel doorman

to get them a carriage. Once they were in the carriage and on their way to St. Mary's Hospital, they discussed their plans for the night.

"How are we going to play this?" Ellie asked. "There are only two of us, and we can't hope to cover all the entrances and exits to the hospital."

"I'm going to position you right outside Roper's window," Clint explained, "and I'm going to spend the night patroling the grounds around the hospital."

"The room only has one window?"

"Yes," Clint said, "and under the circumstances that's one too many. When I was there this afternoon it wasn't even locked."

Ellie shook her head and said, "The Denver police sure are falling down on this one."

"I wouldn't blame all of the Denver police," Clint said. "Inspector Burns is in charge of the situation, and he's the one dictating the quality of protection they're giving Roper."

"Which is nil."

"Exactly as he's planned, no doubt," Clint said, "which is probably another reason why the would-be killer or killers haven't tried for him in the hospital."

"Why?"

"They can't believe how accessible he is," Clint said, opening the door. "They figure if it's that easy, it's got to be a trap!"

FOURTEEN

When they reached the hospital they went inside to see if Sister Ruth were still there.

"I really like Sister Ruth, Clint," Ellie said, "but I really can't understand why a girl as young and as pretty as she is would want to be a nun."

"Maybe you should ask her, Ellie."

"I mean . . . to be celibate for the rest of her life?" She shook her head. Having just come from Clint's bed, she could not even *imagine* what celibacy would be like.

"Maybe you should ask her about that, too."

Ellie looked at him and said, "Do you think she *has* had sex? I mean, are they allowed to be nuns if they've *had* sex first?"

"I don't know, Ellie," Clint said. "You're asking the wrong person."

When they entered they saw a nun sitting at the desk, but her head was down so they didn't know if she was Sister Ruth or not. When they reached the desk she looked up, and they saw that she wasn't. Not unless Ruth had aged about forty years since the last time they'd seen her.

"Can I help you?" the older nun asked.

Clint looked at Ellie, who said, "I was looking for Sister Ruth."

"Well, I am Sister Anne," the nun said. "Can I help you?"

"Uh, no, Sister Ruth is a friend of mine. I just wanted to . . . talk to her."

"At ten minutes after midnight?" the older woman asked. "Isn't it rather late for that? Sister Ruth is a very young woman, you know, and she needs—"

"You see," Clint said, taking Ellie by the shoulders, "I told you Sister Ruth wouldn't be here. Now you can just tell *me* what's bothering you." He smiled at the nun and said, "I'm sorry to have bothered you."

"That's all right. Is this your daughter?"

Clint started to say no but was cut off by Ellie.

"Come on, Dad," she said. "We have to go."

She grabbed Clint by the arm and tugged him away from the desk.

"Dad?" Clint asked outside.

"You started it."

"How did I start it?"

"You used a fatherly tone of voice on me," she said. "Even Sister Anne noticed it."

Clint thought about it for a moment, then said, "I guess I did, didn't I? Sorry."

"Where's that window you want me to sit outside all night?"

Clint had to turn and face the hospital, then take that walk in his mind with Sister Ruth again. "This way."

They went around the left side of the hospital and through a courtyard before Clint felt he had the right window.

"Is this it?" she asked.

He leaned over and peered in the window.

"Yeah, this is it," he said. He looked around the courtyard, shaking his head. "Look at where they put him. Buried in this courtyard, at night like this, this is the easiest room in the hospital to break into."

"Well, like you said, the killers must have felt that way, too—that it was *too* easy."

"Yeah, well, they're going to change their minds, eventually," Clint said, "and when they do, *you'll* be here."

"Me?"

He smiled and said, "Just kidding. After tonight we'll have someone else here."

"How long can we stay on guard?"

"Until he wakes up and tells us what this is all about," Clint said.

"Or until he dies." She said it very quietly, like she didn't *want* to say it, but she knew it *had* to be said.

"Yeah," he said, "that too."

With Ellie in place for the night, Clint began making a circuit of the hospital grounds. Because of the odd construction of the building, walking around it entailed making several blind rights and lefts. Clint had to be careful at each point, and it slowed his progress. Still, better to be safe and slow than walk into the arms of a would-be killer.

On his first trip around the hospital he noticed that there were other buildings behind it. One appeared to be a church. He wondered if the church had the same name—St. Mary's—as the hospital. There were two other buildings, one on either side of the church, but he didn't know what they were. He wondered suddenly where Sister Ruth and the other sisters lived. Maybe that's what one of the buildings was for; and maybe the other one served the same purpose for the priests. Next time he saw Sister Ruth, he'd have to ask her.

Clint expected a quiet night. For someone to try to kill Talbot Roper on this night, the first night he and Ellie were on guard, would have been too much of a coincidence.

He wondered about the people Kit Russell had promised to supply him. If she were to loan him the twins, they'd certainly make impressive-looking guards for Roper. Clint wondered whether they should keep watch over Roper secretly or make it obvious. If they did it secretly, there was a chance they could catch someone making another try at

Roper. There was also a chance someone would make a try and succeed!

On the other hand, if they did it obviously, that would keep away any would-be killers who wanted a second chance, and they'd never find out who had tried to kill him.

Maybe Roper would just wake up and *tell* them who shot him.

Clint hoped Roper would wake up, eventually, even if he had nothing to tell them. At least he could tell Clint what he was working on. If anyone was a good enough detective to find whoever had shot him, it was Roper himself. Even if he didn't know *who* had shot him, he'd have to know *why*.

All he had to do was wake up—*and* survive surgery to remove the bullet that was lodged in his head.

That wasn't too much to ask.

Was it?

As expected—and hoped—the night went by uneventfully.

When Clint returned to Talbot Roper's window, Ellie Lennox was still there and awake—although not *wide* awake, but then neither was he.

"Did you have a nice night?" he asked her.

She rose and rubbed her behind, which was numb and almost frozen after sitting on the ground so long.

"This was one of the longest nights I ever spent," she said. "You owe me a long hot bath and a warm bed."

"You'll get both if you come back to my hotel with me," he said. "Unless you'd rather go home."

"No," she said, "I want you to pay off right away—if not sooner."

"Then let's find a carriage and get going," he said. "I want to get a few hours' sleep before I go and see Kit Russell. Hopefully, she's found some men who'll be willing to do this job for us. I'd like to be free to keep asking some questions.''

''If you're going to see Kit Russell, I'm going with you,'' she said.

''You liked her that much, eh?''

''No,'' she said, folding her arms beneath her breasts, ''but maybe you did.''

FIFTEEN

They went back to the Denver House and took turns bathing in Clint's bathtub. The only reason they didn't bathe together was that the tub was just a tad too small. Also, they would have spent so much time in the tub together that they would have been wrinkled all over by the time they got out.

Of course, there was nothing to stop them from spending time in bed together, which they did. They spent only half an hour making love, though, and then both drifted into a dreamless sleep.

Clint awoke first and debated whether he should wake Ellie or let her sleep. It was almost lunchtime, and he wanted to go and see Kit Russell. He also wanted to go back to Roper's office and talk to Carly Kirkland some more and check to make sure she was all right.

While he was trying to make up his mind, she saved him the trouble by waking up on her own.

"You're dressed!" she said.

"Yes."

"Were you going to wake me?"

"I was thinking about it."

"What are your plans for today?" she asked, rolling over onto her back.

"I'm going to go and see Carly Kirkland—Roper's secretary—and then Kit Russell."

She threw the sheet back and scrambled out of bed. She

would have looked cute doing it even if she weren't naked.

"You think I'm going to let you go and see your other women without me?"

"My 'other women'?"

"Just let me get dressed," she said, and then, "Oh hell!"

"What?"

"I didn't go home, so I've got to wear the same clothes I sat on the ground all night in."

"Well, why don't you go home and change?"

"What's your first stop?"

"I'm picking Kirkland up at her house; then we're going over to Roper's office."

"What's she like?"

"She's a nice young girl."

"All right," Ellie said, "I'll go home and change, you go and see the 'nice young girl,' and I'll meet you at Kit's Place."

"All right," he said, "but don't you think you'd better send word to Pinkerton about why you didn't show up at work today?"

"Oh, hell, I forgot about that!" she said, doing a little jump that made her breasts jiggle.

"I'll see you later this afternoon," he said, heading for the door. "Meet me about four at Kit's."

Clint knocked on the office door before entering, so as not to frighten Carly Kirkland.

"Oh, hi," she said as he came in. She was sitting behind her desk.

"You don't look like you have much to do, Carly."

"I don't," she said with a shrug, "not unless a potential clients walks in, and then I just have to tell them that Mr. Roper isn't here."

"Why keep coming to work then?"

"I don't know," she said. "What would I do if I didn't?"

That was a good question. Apparently she didn't have much of a life outside of this office.

"Don't you have any friends you could spend some time with?"

"Not really," she said. "I just got to Denver a year ago and haven't had much time to make friends."

Clint didn't know what to tell her.

"Have you seen Mr. Roper?" she asked.

"Yes, I have. His condition hasn't changed."

"How did it go with Inspector Burns?"

Clint told her about his talk with the inspector and about his decision to try and arrange some private security for Roper.

"You mean you're hiring some help?"

"Not exactly. I'm going to see some people today about volunteering."

"Volunteering?"

"If it happens, I'll explain it to you," Clint said. "Carly, I think that under the circumstances, you shouldn't stay around here alone."

"What circumstances?"

"Well, it's a bad neighborhood, and there's really nothing for you to do here."

"You're worried about me, aren't you?"

"Well, not worried, exactly . . ."

"Tell me the truth, Clint."

He hesitated a moment, then said, "Well, all right. We still don't know *why* Roper was shot. It could be that whoever shot him wanted something and didn't get it."

"And they might come back here for it?"

"It's unlikely," Clint said, "because if they were going to do it they probably would have done so long before now, but just to be on the safe side I think you should close up the office until . . . until the situation resolves itself."

"You mean until he either wakes up or dies, don't you?" she asked.

"Yes," he said, "that's what I mean."

Carly Kirkland thought about that for a few moments, then placed her hands flat on the desk and pushed to her feet.

"All right," she said, "I'll take your advice. I've been thinking about this, and just because I've worked here for three months is no reason for me to get killed—not when I won't even know why."

"That's very good thinking, Carly."

"You don't think I'm just being a coward, do you?"

"No," Clint said, "I think you're being very sensible. I'll close up for you. I just want to have another look around."

"Fine," she said. She started for the door, then turned around and asked, "Do you think it will be all right if I go to the hospital to see him?"

"Sure," he said. "Just let me clear it with the inspector, okay?"

"Thanks."

"I'll be in touch." As she opened the door he asked, "Do you want to wait for me to walk you out?"

"No," she said, "I'll be fine. I just hope you find something here that will help you figure out who shot Mr. Roper."

"I hope so too, Carly."

SIXTEEN

Kit Russell looked up from her desk when the knock came at her door.

"Come in."

A man entered and walked directly to the desk.

"Christopher," she said to her maitre d', "what have you got for me?"

"The report on Clint Adams, madame," he said.

"Give it to me."

He handed her a folder.

"You put this together very quickly, didn't you?"

He smiled and said, "That's what you asked me to do, isn't it?"

"Yes," she said, "and you always do what I ask you to do, don't you, Christopher?"

"We all do, madame."

"Did you talk to Maurice and Dutch?"

"Yes."

"And?"

"Maurice agreed."

"And Dutch?"

Christopher shook his head. "He said his place is here, keeping you safe."

"Dear Dutch. Did you speak to Max?"

"Yes," Christopher said, "and he agreed. So did Henry."

"Henry?"

"He volunteered."

"How are *we* fixed, Christopher?" she asked. "Can we survive without them for a while?"

"We can do without a waiter and a bartender for a while," Christopher said. "Probably without Maurice as a bouncer, too. He'd rather be working outside somewhere, anyway."

"Good."

"Uh, how long will they be away, madame?" Christopher asked.

"I don't know, Christopher," she said. "As long as Mr. Roper needs them."

"I see."

"Let's put Dutch inside and someone else on the outside, Christopher," she said. "I'd feel better with Dutch on the inside."

"Yes, madame."

"How does this look, Christopher?" she asked, indicating the folder.

"Very impressive, madame," Christopher said. "He is who he says he is and much more."

"Interesting," she said.

"Yes, it is," Christopher said, "very interesting reading."

"Thank you, Christopher," Kit Russell said. "Tell Maurice, Max, and Henry that I'll expect them to speak with Mr. Adams when he arrives."

"Yes, madame," the maitre d' said, "I will tell them."

"I'll let you know when he's here."

As Christopher opened the door to leave, Kit Russell opened the folder and began reading.

Clint sat down behind Roper's desk and sat back in the chair. For all that Carly Kirkland wanted to help, looking through Roper's desk was something that Clint should have done on his own. Now that he was alone in the office, he intended to go through it again, piece by piece.

After half an hour he had gone through all the drawers and was ready to go over the top of the desk, which was a holy mess. There were papers strewn all about, and it had been that way even before Clint and Carly had searched it the first time.

He didn't know what kind of order—if any—the papers should be in, so he simply began to stack them so that he could go through them in an orderly fashion. When he had them stacked they formed a sheath about half an inch thick. He found that odd, since Roper had reportedly had very few cases of late. Among the papers in the stack were some newspaper articles, some telegram flimsies, and what looked like old files.

Clint began going through the stack.

He found a flimsy copy of the telegram Roper had sent to him; he found pages torn from several newspapers; he found a telegram to Roper from a railroad detective saying that he'd be arriving in town today.

There were plenty of other things to read in that stack of papers, but in the end the only things he separated from the rest were the newspaper pages and the telegram from the railroad detective.

The newspaper pages all had a particular article in common. It was about a shipment of $200,000.00 in gold that was stolen from a train in Texas. In each case the robbery had been given major coverage in the newspaper. The papers were all a month old.

He sat back in the chair, holding a newspaper page in one hand and the telegram in the other.

Would someone shoot Talbot Roper because he was about to get involved in looking for a gold shipment that was stolen a month ago?

He read the telegram again:

ROPER

ARRIVING DENVER OCTOBER 5. STAYING

AT ST. REGIS HOTEL. NEED TO TALK. COME AND SEE ME OR I WILL COME AND SEE YOU.

It was signed by Heck Thomas, a railroad detective whom Clint had worked with once upon a time, a few years back. In fact, Heck Thomas was the best railroad detective Clint Adams had ever known. If it wasn't for Talbot Roper, Heck Thomas may have been the best detective of any kind that Clint Adams knew.

The fact that a railroad detective was interested in talking to Roper and that Roper had saved clippings of a railroad robbery made Clint think that there was a very strong chance Roper was about to become involved in looking for that $200,000.00 in gold.

If it was still missing.

Clint folded the clippings and the telegram and got up from the desk, leaving it considerably neater than when he first sat down. He had decided to find out if that shipment was still missing.

And who better to ask than Heck Thomas, railroad detective?

SEVENTEEN

When Clint walked into the lobby of the St. Regis Hotel he knew he was going to be late in meeting Ellie at Kit's Place. He hoped that Ellie and Kit would be able to get along without him.

At the desk Clint asked, "What room is Mr. Heck Thomas in?"

"Sir?"

"Heck Thomas?"

"I'll have to check, sir," the clerk said haughtily. Clint hated such men.

"You do that."

The clerk did some checking in his registry and then said, "No, we don't seem to have a guest by that name, sir." There was no sympathy in his tone at all.

"Would you check and see if he has a reservation—or if he had one?"

The man gave Clint an impatient look, then nodded and went through a file.

"Oh, yes, he did have a reservation."

"For today?"

"Yes."

"And he's not here?"

The clerk heaved a put-upon sigh and said, "Obviously not."

"All right," Clint said, "let me describe the man to you.

He's tall, heavy through the chest, he's got a full jaw, probably needs a shave—"

"Oh," the clerk said, "him."

"Then he was here?"

"Oh, yes," the clerk said, looking uncomfortable. "Oh, yes, he was here."

Clint waited a few moments, and when the clerk didn't say anything else, he said, "Well?"

"I . . . think you'd better talk to our manager," the clerk said. "I'll get him for you."

"You do that."

The clerk left the desk and returned a couple of minutes later with a tall, gray-haired man who looked agitated.

"Are you a friend of Heck Thomas?" the man demanded.

"I'm looking for him," Clint said carefully.

"He was here last night," the manager said.

"And?"

"And he didn't like the room we gave him," the manager replied. "He was abusive, and he damaged the room."

"Why?"

"Because he's crazy, that's why!" the man said. "I had to call security to get him out of here."

"Your security man threw him out?"

"Four."

"Four what?"

"It took four security men to throw him out."

"I beg your pardon," Clint said, wanting to laugh, "but if Heck Thomas didn't want to leave, not even four of your security men could have thrown him out."

"Well . . . he left," the manager said, "but I want to find him."

"What for?"

"What for? To sue him for the damages! And he broke one of my men's arms."

"So you don't know where he is?"

"No."

"Well, thanks anyway."

"Hey, wait," the manager said. "If you find him you'll let me know, right?"

Clint turned around and very deliberately looked at the hotel manager. "Wrong," he said.

"Why not?" the man demanded.

Clint grinned and said, "Because he's a friend of mine, like you said."

Clint left the hotel, thinking about Heck Thomas. It did not surprise him that Heck had trashed his hotel room. The man had a special way about him when he was riled. Something must have happened to set him off, though. Heck was not given to unprovoked fits of anger. When he hurt someone—like a security man—it was usually because they put their hands on him first.

After Clint left the St. Regis he had two options. He could go to Kit's Place and talk to Kit Russell, or he could go looking for Heck Thomas. If he knew Heck, he wouldn't be at the Denver House, or any hotel like it or the St. Regis. He'd be in a somewhat less expensive hotel, where the room suited him more and where the people who worked there weren't looking down their noses at him.

He decided to go and talk to Kit first and get Roper's security set up. Once he was sure Roper was safe, he could continue trying to find out why he was shot and by whom. Part of that would be talking to Heck Thomas.

He had a feeling he knew where he'd find him.

EIGHTEEN

When Clint arrived at Kit's Place there was a different man at the door. He wondered if that meant that the doorman, Dutch, was going to be one of the men used for Roper's security.

As he approached the front door, the man moved in front of it and said, "The restaurant's not open yet."

This man was not as tall as Dutch, but he had wide shoulders and a deep chest, and he'd be almost as difficult to get by as Dutch.

"My name is Clint Adams."

The man relaxed visibly and said, "Oh, yes, Mr. Adams. You can go in, sir."

"Thank you. Uh, is there a young lady in there with Miss Russell?"

"Yes, sir," the man said. "I believe her name is Miss Lennox?"

"That's her."

"She arrived some time ago."

"All right, thank you."

The man opened the door and Clint entered. There were a couple of men sweeping the floor and another two men setting up chairs. He saw movement from the corner of his eye, and then Dutch stepped into view.

"Mr. Adams," he said. "Follow me, please."

"Sure, Dutch," Clint said. "Lead the way."

He followed Dutch to Kit Russell's office, as he had

followed his brother the day before. Dutch knocked on the door and opened it, then stepped aside to allow Clint to enter.

Kit Russell was seated behind her desk, and Ellie Lennox was in a chair across from her. Both women seemed to be laughing, and both had cups of coffee or tea in front of them.

"Ah, Clint," Kit said. "Come in and join us."

"Nice to see you made it," Ellie said.

"Dutch, ask the others to join us."

"Yes, ma'am."

Clint heard the door close behind him.

"Tea?" Kit asked.

"Why not?" Clint said. "Sorry I'm late."

"What kept you?" Ellie asked.

"I had to go to Roper's office and look it over again," he explained.

"Did you find anything?" Kit asked.

Clint approached her desk and accepted the cup of tea she handed him.

"Yeah, maybe I did," he said, "but I have to talk to a man first."

"Who?"

He sipped his tea and looked at Kit over the rim.

"Oh, I see," she said. "You don't trust me."

"I don't trust anyone," he said. "I don't even *know* you."

"But you'll accept my help?" she asked. Her color was rising, as was her anger.

"Don't get so angry with me, Miss Russell," he said. "Tell me you didn't have me checked out."

"I *did* have you checked out."

"Well, I don't have your resources," Clint said, "so I have to do it my way."

Kit stared at Clint for a few moments until Ellie said, "He's right, Kit."

Kit? Apparently the two women had become very friendly while waiting for him to arrive.

"I know he is," Kit said, and she sat down.

"Do you have some men for me?" Clint asked.

"Yes."

"Good ones?"

"Yes."

"Dutch?"

"Dutch refused," she said. "He feels he's needed more here."

"To protect you?"

"Yes."

Kit Russell was apparently more than she appeared to be, but that wasn't his problem right now.

There was a knock on the door and it opened. Three men walked in. Clint recognized two of them. One was Dutch's twin brother, and the other was Henry, the waiter who had served him and Ellie their dinner the night before.

He turned and looked at Kit. "A waiter?"

"Henry spent eleven years as a mercenary, his many talents for hire to anyone who could afford him."

"And now he's a waiter?"

"He's retired."

"Is he?"

"Come in, boys," Kit said. "This is Clint Adams. He will explain what this is all about. If you agree to be part of it, you will be answerable to him."

The three men came forward and formed a semicircle around her desk.

"This is Maurice, Dutch's twin brother. Dutch is the polished one—that's why he usually works the door. Maurice, on the other hand, likes to use his hands, which is why he's the bouncer."

"Can he use his head?"

"When I have to," Maurice said, answering the question

himself. "Just because I like to break heads doesn't make me dumb."

"No," Clint said, matching the man's stare, "it doesn't."

"Henry Dux has many talents," Kit said. She pronounced it "Dukes."

"Not the least of which is that he's an excellent waiter," Clint said.

Henry smiled, and it was hard for Clint to imagine this portly, benign-looking man as a mercenary.

"This is Max Gorton, my bartender," Kit said, indicating the third man. He was built like a prizefighter and had the face to match. There was a scar through his right eyebrow and another that caused the right corner of his mouth to twist upward. He'd grown a little thick around the middle, but it was a hard thickness. His arms and legs were like tree trunks.

"Fighter?" Clint asked.

"For twenty years," Max said. "I was never a champ, but I was never knocked off my feet either."

"I can believe it."

It was a motley-seeming crew for a woman like Kit Russell to have put together. Given that Henry was a mercenary before he was a waiter and Max was a fighter before he was a bartender, Clint wondered what Kit was before she was a restaurant owner.

And he noticed that no one had said what Maurice—and his twin brother, Dutch—were before they became a bouncer and a doorman.

Clint wondered what other kinds of characters Kit Russell had working for her. He also wondered what Talbot Roper knew about his ladyfriend's past.

"Will these three be enough?" Kit asked.

"If they're willing," Clint said, "I think they'll do very nicely."

"What is it we have to do?" Max asked.

Clint explained about Roper's hospital room being badly protected.

"The three of you will have to stand guard each night," he finished, "and make sure no one gets to him and finishes the job."

Kit looked at each man in turn. "Are you boys willing?"

"For Roper? Sure," Max said.

"I'm in," Henry said.

"I'll do it," Maurice said, "but not for Roper. I'm doing it for you, ma'am."

Kit graced him with a dazzling smile and said, "Thank you, Maurice."

"When do we start?" Max asked.

"Tonight will be your first night on guard."

"Until when?" Maurice asked.

Everyone in the room exchanged glances, and no one had to answer that question.

NINETEEN

That night Clint accompanied the three men to the hospital and together they picked out the best positions and routes. It was decided that Henry would position himself by Roper's window, Max would cover the rear of the hospital, and Maurice the front.

Before placing them, though, Clint went inside to see if Sister Ruth were on duty, and he found her behind the desk.

"Hello, Sister."

She looked up and smiled when she saw him.

"Hello, Clint," she said, then closed one eye and pointed her finger at him. "It was you looking for me last night, wasn't it?"

"Yes," he said, "me and Ellie Lennox."

"The lady from Pinkerton?"

"That's right."

"Father and daughter?"

Clint laughed with her and said, "That was somebody's idea of a joke."

"What can I do for you tonight?"

"Would you be able to step outside for a moment?"

"Sure," she said, coming around the desk. "What for?"

"I want you meet some people."

She walked to the door with him, and when they stepped outside she saw the three men standing there.

"I wanted you to meet these three gentlemen so that if you see them hanging around the hospital you don't send for the police. This is Max, Maurice, and Henry, and they're all here to protect Talbot Roper."

"A pleasure to meet you, gentlemen."

All three men didn't seem to know what to do in the presence of a nun, so they nodded and shuffled their feet and stared at the ground.

Clint walked back inside with her.

"Will they be here all night?" she asked.

"Yes."

"What about the daytime?"

"I don't think anyone will try anything during the day," Clint said. "The original attack was at night, and I think that's their style."

"Well, I'm sure he'll be safe now with his friends around him."

"Is there any change in his condition that you know of?"

"Not that I know of, Clint," she said. "I'm sorry."

"I hope he comes out of it soon," Clint said.

"So do I," Sister Ruth said.

"If any of those men need explaining, Sister, can I count on you to vouch for them?"

"Of course," she said. "I'll do whatever I can to help."

"Thank you for your help, Sister."

Clint went outside and said to the three men, "Take up your positions."

"We stay put until daylight?" Max asked.

"That's right," Clint said, "until daylight."

"Let's do it," Henry said.

"If anything happens," Clint said, "one of you come to my hotel to get me."

They all nodded and went to take up their positions.

Clint left the hospital and headed for his hotel, where Ellie was waiting for him. He felt a little guilty going to a warm bed—and warm body—while the other three men would be staying up and out all night, but he needed his sleep so he would be wide awake during the day, to continue his investigation.

It hadn't been much of an investigation up to now, but tomorrow he was going to start pushing for answers.

Roper was protected, so now Clint could stop worrying about him and start looking in earnest for whoever shot him.

When Clint entered his room he could hear Ellie's even breathing from the bed. It wasn't late, but she must have fallen asleep while waiting for him.

He removed his gunbelt and then undressed. They had stopped for dinner after leaving Kit's and had then come back here and made love. He had told her about wanting to find Heck Thomas, because although he didn't trust Kit Russell—because he didn't know her—he did know and trust Ellie.

"I like Kit, Clint," Ellie had told him over dinner.

"Maybe I do, too, El," he said, "but we can't trust her, not yet."

Clint had left her awake and dressed when he went to meet the three men at the hospital. His impression had been that she was going to go out and take care of some business. He had no way of knowing if she had done that or fallen right back to sleep.

Naked, he slid into bed next to her. Her hip was warm against his and, when she felt him in bed with her she moved, rolling over and throwing her leg over him.

"You're back," she said.

"Yes."

He put his arm around her, and she snuggled up against him.

"Did you go out?" he asked.

"Yes."

"Did you get done what you wanted to get done?"

"Yes," she answered sleepily.

"Good."

"And you?"

"Yes."

"Then we have all night to ourselves?" she asked. Her hand snaked down over one of his thighs.

"Yes," he said, "but I have to get up early in the morning."

"What for?"

"To start looking for Heck Thomas."

"Where will you look?"

"Roper's office," Clint said. "Chances are Heck doesn't know Roper's in the hospital. He'll go to his old office and then track him to the new one. I'll be there waiting for him."

"Well," Ellie said, "if you miss him there you could always go to his hotel."

"If I knew where it was."

"I do," she said, and there was a supressed giggle in her tone.

He looked down at her, barely able to make out her features in the dark, and said, "You do?"

"That's why I went out," she said.

"How did you find him?"

"I'm a detective," she said, "remember?"

"What's the name of the hotel?"

"Huh-uh."

"You're not going to tell me?"

"Nope," she said. Her hand slid from his thigh and closed around his semi-erect penis. "Not until you've earned it."

He ran one hand up and down her back and asked, "And what do I have to do to earn it?"

She laughed, a deep, throaty, sexy sound, and said, "Just lie still."

She slid down between his legs and slid the length of him into her mouth. Holding him around the base of his penis, she began to bob her head up and down, sucking him noisily. He lifted his buttocks off the bed as he felt the explosion coming and then groaned out loud as he ejaculated into her mouth. . . .

Later she still refused to tell him the name of the hotel, so he decided turnabout was fair play.

He slid down between her legs and began to lap at her, running his tongue up and down her moist slit, only occasionally flicking her clit with his tongue. Finally he centered his attention there, working on her until she was moaning and writhing in anticipation of her release . . . and then he stopped.

"Ooh, no, don't stop, don't . . ."

"What's the name of the hotel?" he asked.

"Oh, you bastard!" she said. "Finish me and I'll tell you."

"Tell me now," he said. He leaned over and blew on her clit. "What hotel?"

"God," she moaned, "the Prince Charles, damn you. Now finish me!"

He smiled and said, "With pleasure."

TWENTY

Clint rose early the next morning. Since Ellie had found out the name of Heck Thomas's hotel for him, he decided to try and catch Heck there early. Heck had had one day to find Roper's office, but Clint had already taken Carly out of there so there would have been no one to let him in. If he had let himself in, there was still nothing there to tell him where Roper was.

If Heck hadn't found Roper by day's end, he'd have to go back to square one today and start at his office. Clint hoped to find him before he left.

The Prince Charles was a considerable distance down the ladder from the Denver House, despite its royal-sounding name.

Clint entered and approached the desk, hoping that Heck had not had some trouble here, as well as the St. Regis.

"Yeah?" the clerk said. "Help ya?" He was a skinny man wearing a shirt that was badly frayed around the collar and cuffs.

"I'd like to know what room Heck Thomas is in."

"Who?"

Clint closed his eyes for a moment and repeated, "Heck Thomas? I understand he's a guest here."

"Lemme check."

When the man made no move to check, Clint realized what he was waiting for. He took out a dollar and put it on the counter.

"Lemme check," the man said again. He looked through the registry and said, "Yeah, he checked in."

"What's his room number?"

"I can't tell you that."

"I'm not giving you anymore money, friend," Clint said.

"Hotel policy," the man said, "for the benefit of the guests. I can't tell you his room number."

"Is his key still in his box?"

The man said, "Yes."

Clint had been hoping that the man would turn around and look, at least giving Clint some idea of what floor Heck was on.

"You didn't look."

"I been a desk clerk for a long time, friend," the man said. "I know whether my guests are in or not."

"All right," Clint said, "thanks."

"Another dollar gets you his room number."

Clint smiled and said, "I'll just sit in the lobby and wait for him."

"You can't sit in the lobby."

"Why not?"

"I can't let you."

Clint grinned tightly at the man and said, "Are you going to stop me?"

The man backed away from Clint's look, but before he could try to answer another voice cut loudly through the tension.

"Clint Adams, is that you?"

Clint knew the voice, and he turned to face Heck Thomas.

"Heck, you old dog."

"It is you," Heck said, bearing down on Clint. "What the hell are you doing here?"

"Have you had breakfast?" Clint asked as the two men shook hands.

"Hell no, I just got up."

"Let's go and get some, and we'll talk about what I'm doing here and what you're doing here."

"What do you know about what I'm doing here?"

"All I know is that it's connected to what I'm doing here."

"And what's that?"

"I'm trying to find out who shot Talbot Roper."

"Roper, shot?" Heck repeated. "Is he dead?"

"No," Clint said, and then added, "not yet."

"What's that mean?"

"Let's go someplace, Heck," Clint said. "This hotel lobby is not exactly the place to talk about this."

"This hotel ain't the place to talk about anything," Heck said. "I seen better places in small Mexican towns—with better service."

They left the hotel and walked until they found a restaurant. They went inside and were seated.

"Now what's going on?" Heck asked after the waiter had gone to put in their orders. "Who shot Talbot Roper and why?"

"I don't know who," Clint said, "but I was hoping you could tell me why."

"Why me?"

"Because nobody knows what Roper was working on when he was shot," Clint said, "and he's not awake to tell us. I think that whatever brought you to Denver is the reason he was shot."

"You don't know anything about it?" Heck asked. He eyed Clint suspiciously.

"About what? All I know is that Roper asked me to come to Denver."

"You never spoke to him?"

"I never had the chance," Clint said. "He was in the hospital when I got here." Clint waited a beat and then added, "He was shot in the head, Heck."

"Jesus . . ."

The waiter came with coffee then, and both leaned back and fell silent while he put it down. Heck seemed to be taking the moment to consider what he was going to say next. Clint was wondering whether or not Heck was going to lie to him. If this was about the stolen money, the chances were that he would.

"Clint," he said, after the waiter had left, "it's good to see you after all this time, it really is, but if you don't know what's going on, I don't know if I want to let you in on it. I mean, friendship's one thing, but business is another. I just have to—"

Clint decided to save Heck from lying.

"Let me take a guess," he said. "Are we talking about something in the neighborhood of two hundred thousand dollars?"

Heck stiffened and looked around to see if anyone had heard Clint. "I thought you didn't know anything?"

Clint took out the newspaper clippings he had in his pocket and dropped them on the table.

"I found those on Roper's desk," Clint said. "Now do you want to tell me what the hell is going on?"

TWENTY-ONE

Heck talked through lunch.

The $200,000.00 had been stolen from a Texas & Pacific train a month before, and two Wells Fargo guards had been killed. A reward was being offered by both the railroad and Wells Fargo.

"The total reward comes to forty thousand dollars."

"One-fifth of what was stolen?" Clint asked. "Isn't that high?"

Heck held up two fingers. "Two men were killed. Wells Fargo doesn't take that lightly."

"You're representing the railroad?"

"Yes."

"They don't want to pay the reward."

"Not if they don't have to."

"And Wells Fargo?"

"They'd rather not pay either," Heck said. "That's only natural for both of them."

"Who's representing them?"

"An outside man," Heck said. "Feller named Jake Benteen."

"Benteen?"

"You know him?"

"Yes," Clint said, "but he's a bounty hunter."

"He's branching out."

"He used to have a female partner."

"Lacy Blake? I understand they parted company."

"Do you know why?"

"No. Does it have some bearing—"

"No," Clint said, "they're both just friends. So Benteen is working to save Wells Fargo their reward, you're working for the railroad. What's Roper working for?"

"Himself," Heck said. "He sent for all the information we had."

"You mean he's after the reward?"

"Right."

"So why did you come to see him?"

"To offer him a deal."

"I get it," Clint said. "You're afraid he'll find the gold and collect the whole reward."

"Right."

"What about Wells Fargo?"

"What about them?"

"Are they worried too?"

"They're taking normal steps to protect the reward, but they'd prefer having the men caught who killed two of their men."

Clint toyed with the food in his plate for a few moments.

"Heck, who else is looking for the gold?"

"A lot of people," Heck said. "They're coming out of the woodwork."

"How come I didn't hear about this?"

"Knowing you, I'd say you were moving around, probably had your nose buried in someone else's business."

"Could this be why Roper was shot?" Clint asked.

"What do you mean?"

"Do you think there could be someone who's looking for that gold who thought there was a good chance Roper would get there first?"

"So they tried to kill him to get him out of the way?" Heck said.

"That's what I'm getting at."

"Forty thousand dollars is a lot of money," Heck said. "It's possible."

"Do you know of any other detectives from Denver who might be looking for that gold?"

"I know some cutthroats, some low-life bounty hunters, and a lot of amateurs who are looking for that money," Heck said, "but I don't know of anyone from Denver who'd be willing to kill for it. Hell, even Pinkerton's looking for it."

"What?" Clint dropped his utensils onto his plate and they landed with a bang.

"Yeah," Heck said, "I heard Pinkerton was sending out an operative to look for the gold, but not even he would kill for it."

"Do you know who Pinkerton assigned?"

"No, why?"

"I'm good friends with a Pinkerton operative," Clint said, "and she didn't say a word about it."

Heck shrugged. "Do you think we can get a beer in here?"

"At this hour?" Clint said. "I sure as hell hope so."

After they had finished their breakfast—and the beer they'd had to pry out of the waiter—they left the restaurant.

"Heck, what are your plans now?"

"I'm heading back to Texas to try again to find that gold," Heck said. "Whoever these thieves were, they've covered their tracks extremely well."

"When are you leaving?"

"In the morning."

"Want some company?"

Heck frowned and said, "You're not interested in the reward, are you?"

"I'm interested in who shot Talbot Roper," Clint said. "I'm starting to think that maybe the man who pulled the trigger left Denver long before I got here."

"And you think you'll find him in Texas?"

"I think I've got a better chance of finding him there than here."

Heck shrugged and said, "I'm going to try and get a seat on as early a train as possible."

"Get two," Clint said. "Leave a message at my hotel with the time, and I'll meet you at the station."

"What are you going to do now?"

"Right now? I'm going to talk to Allan Pinkerton."

"Do you know Pinkerton?"

"I know him."

"Like him?"

"Nobody likes him."

"That's what I've heard," Heck said. "All right, Clint. We'll work on this together, and if we find the gold, you'll get the reward."

"I'll take a percentage," Clint said. "If we find it together, it'll be as much your doing as mine. I don't think I'd be entitled to the entire amount. Besides, part of your job is to make sure the reward *doesn't* get paid out, isn't it?"

"No," he said, "part of my job is to make sure that the reward isn't paid out unnecessarily. There's a difference."

"I see," Clint said. "All right, we'll cross that bridge when we come to it."

"Did you go through Roper's office?"

"Twice," Clint said. "That's how I came up with the information on the train robbery."

"So there's no doubt in your mind that this is the case he was working on when he was shot."

"He probably hadn't started working on it yet," Clint said, "but I didn't see any indication of another case. I feel pretty safe in assuming that this is it."

"All right," Heck Thomas said, "maybe we can both get what we want out of this."

"I hope so," Clint said, "and maybe we can put away

some people who think killing is a way to get rich."

Heck grinned and said, "I hope so."

After leaving Heck, who was going right to the train station to try and get those tickets, Clint headed for Allan Pinkerton's office.

He couldn't help wondering if Ellie Lennox was the operative Pinkerton had assigned to find the gold. If she was, then there was a question as to why she was waiting around for Roper to wake up and why she was offering to help Clint.

Would Ellie do that? Try and use him like that?

Maybe she was the one he should have been going to see.

TWENTY-TWO

Clint did not have to wait long to get in to see Allan Pinkerton, which should have told him something. The man was just as he remembered: pink skinned like a baby, with snow-white hair, eyebrows, and muttonchops.

"Clint, my boy," he said, rising from his chair behind his desk.

Clint stopped short. He knew he should turn around and walk out again. Allan Pinkerton had called him a lot of things over the years, but "Clint, my boy," was never one of them.

"Have a seat, have a seat," Pinkerton said. "It's fine to see you, lad. What are you doing in town?"

"I was looking for whoever shot Talbot Roper." Clint didn't bother taking a seat.

"I know about that, of course," Pinkerton said. "Terrible thing. Roper and I never did see eye to eye, but I would never have wished this on him."

"I'm sure," Clint said.

"You said you *were* looking for the man who shot Talbot Roper. Have you found him?"

"No, I've just come to the conclusion that the man is no longer in Denver."

"Where is he, then?"

"Texas."

"What would he be doing in Texas?"

"Looking for two hundred thousand dollars in gold, I imagine—just like you."

"Gold?"

"Come on, Pinkerton," Clint said. "Who did you assign to try and find the gold?"

Pinkerton leaned back in his chair and said, "Why would I tell you that?"

"Maybe because I asked nicely?"

"I'll tell you what," Pinkerton said. "I'll tell you who I assigned and then take them *off* the assignment if you'll take it for me."

"What do I get in return?"

"Five thousand dollars—if you find the gold."

"And you get the other thirty-five?" Clint said. "Why don't I just find it for myself?"

"You're not interested in the gold," Pinkerton said, "you're interested in finding out who shot you friend."

"So then why would I take your deal?"

"Because you're going to go out there anyway," Pinkerton said, "and you might as well pick up some expense money."

"I'd love to lie to you, Pinkerton, and tell you yes, just so you'll tell me who you assigned, but I can't do that. I can't lie to you. I have to tell you the truth. That deal stinks."

Pinkerton frowned. "What the hell do you want, Adams?"

"That's more like it," Clint said. "That's the Allan Pinkerton I'm used to."

"Get to the dammed point!"

"You're after the reward," Clint said, "and I'm going to get there before you—unless you tell me who you assigned to the case."

"Wait a minute," Pinkerton said. "Do you think—are you implying that whoever I assigned to the case shot Talbot Roper?"

"I'm not implying anything," Clint said. "Did you know that Roper was looking for the gold?"

"I knew he was *about* to start looking for the gold," Pinkerton said, "but for Chrissake, that doesn't mean I had him shot."

"You knew he'd get there before any of your people."

"Maybe," Pinkerton said.

"Do you have anyone who's half the detective Roper is?" Clint asked.

Pinkerton's jaw tightened, and he said through clenched teeth, "No."

"Do you have any operatives who'd go so far as to shoot Roper to keep him from getting there first?"

Pinkerton hesitated just a fraction of a second before saying, "No."

"Do you know all your operatives well?"

"You know better than that," Pinkerton said. "I know very few of them personally. Bill takes care of that."

"Bill" was William Pinkerton, Allan's son.

"Is he around?"

"Adams," Pinkerton said, leaning forward. His face was pinker than usual. "None of my people shot Talbot Roper, either by my order or otherwise."

"How good a chance do you think you have of getting to the gold now that Roper's out of the way?"

"A *damned* good chance!"

"There are others involved, you know," Clint said. "Heck Thomas, Jake Benteen . . . I think you're going to bring up the rear, Pinkerton. I don't think you're going to get within *smelling* distance of that gold—or of the reward money."

"I think it's time for you to leave, Adams!"

"I agree with you, Allan," Clint said. "It's getting a little close in here."

"Out!"

Clint left, no better off than when he had arrived—but, then, he was no worse off, either.

It was time to talk to Ellie Lennox herself.

"Adams!"

Clint was on his way out, and he turned to see who had called his name. It was William Pinkerton, bearing down on him with a mighty frown—that is, William *meant* it to be a mighty frown. To Clint it just looked silly. As far as Clint was concerned, William Pinkerton was a forty-odd man who had not managed to get out from beneath his father's thumb.

"What are you doing here?"

"I just had a very interesting conversation with your father."

"Did you upset him?"

Clint hesitated, then said, "Yeah, I believe I did. I kind of enjoyed it, too."

"What did you say?"

"We talked about gold, Willy," Clint said, lowering his voice so that William had to lean forward to hear him. "Two hundred thousand dollars in gold—which you Pinkertons will never see. Bye, Willy."

He left William Pinkerton standing in the hall and hoped he was as upset as his father.

TWENTY-THREE

When Clint got back to his hotel he found two things waiting for him: Ellie Lennox and a message from Heck Thomas.

Clint was standing at the desk, reading the message from Heck, when Ellie came up behind him.

"Can we talk?" Ellie asked.

He looked over his shoulder at her and folded the message from Heck Thomas. Heck had managed to get a nine-o'clock train, which suited Clint just fine.

"About what?"

"I saw you today."

"Where?"

"At Pinkerton's."

"Did you talk to him?"

"No," she said. "I came here to talk to you."

"Let's go into the dining room."

They walked to the dining room in silence and waited until they were seated to speak.

"Clint, I want to go with you."

"Where?"

"To look for the gold."

"So you're the one Pinkerton assigned," he said. "I was hoping—"

"No, you don't understand," she said, cutting him off. "I'm *not* the one he assigned. I wanted the case, but he wouldn't give it to me."

"Who did he give it to?"

"I don't know," Ellie said. "In fact, I don't think anyone knows but Allan Pinkerton."

"Not even his son?"

"I don't think even William knows."

"Ellie," Clint said, "I'm leaving tomorrow morning with Heck Thomas. We cut a deal, and taking you with me would negate the deal."

"But you and I could find the gold."

"Maybe we could," he said, "but I've already come to an agreement with Heck. I'm sorry."

"I thought we were friends," she said.

"Don't do that, Ellie."

"I thought we were more than friends." She was hurt, and she was talking without thinking.

"Ellie . . ."

"Never mind, Clint Adams," she said, standing up, "I'll find that gold on my own, without you and without any help from Allan Pinkerton."

With that, she turned and stalked out of the dining room. He started to follow her into the lobby, but as she went out the front door and turned left, someone came from the right and entered.

It was Sister Ruth.

She spotted him and quickly crossed the lobby to him.

"I'm glad I found you here, Clint," she said, looking and sounding either excited or agitated.

"What is it?" Clint asked. "Has something happened to Roper?"

"Yes," she said, "something wonderful, something miraculous! He's awake."

"Awake?" Clint asked. "You mean, alert?"

"Yes."

"With a bullet lodged in his head?"

"Yes," Sister Ruth said. "The doctor wants to take him into surgery while he's strong, but Roper said no."

"No?"

"He wants to talk to you before he agrees."

"That's crazy!"

"Perhaps, but I came here to get you so that you could talk to him quickly."

"Let's go, Sister," he said, taking her arm. "The quicker we get there, the quicker we can get him into surgery."

When Clint entered Talbot Roper's room it was filled with nurses and doctors. He recognized Doctor Frakes immediately, and the doctor was talking earnestly to Tal Roper.

Roper was still lying on his back, but his eyes were open, and when he saw Clint his eyes widened.

Doctor Frakes also saw Clint.

"Mr. Adams, could you talk some sense into your friend, please? We *must* get him into surgery as soon as possible."

"I'll try, Doctor."

Clint moved to Roper's bedside.

"Tal, what are you trying to do?"

"Clear the room, Clint," Roper said. His voice was so low Clint didn't quite hear him.

"What?"

"Clear the room," Roper said. "After we talk, they can take me to surgery."

Clint knew enough not to argue with his friend.

"Doctor, he wants the room cleared."

"This is madness!"

"The faster you clear the room, the faster you can have him in surgery. Get everyone out!"

The doctor hesitated only a moment before saying, "All right, everyone out!"

In a matter of seconds, the room was cleared except for Clint and Roper.

"All right, Tal," Clint said, leaning over his injured friend, "they're gone. What is it?"

Talking seemed a chore for the injured detective, so he chose as few words as possible.

"Whiskey Bent," he said.

Clint heard him, but he'd never heard of anyplace called Whiskey Bent.

"Where is Whiskey Bent, Tal?"

Roper parted his lips to speak, then had to wet them before he could say, "Texas."

"Texas?" Clint repeated. "Are you saying that the gold is in Whiskey Bent, Texas?"

Roper wet his lips again and said, "Place to start."

"I've got it, Tal," Clint said, putting his hand on the man's shoulder. "Whiskey Bent, Texas, is the place to start looking. Now tell me, who shot you?"

Roper closed his eyes, and for a moment Clint thought he wouldn't open them again, but he did.

"Too dark," he finally said, "too damn dark . . ."

Clint decided there had been enough talking. He hurried to the door and found Doctor Frakes out in the hall.

"He's all yours, Doctor," Clint said.

"Let's get him to surgery," Frakes shouted to his people. "Now, damn it!"

TWENTY-FOUR

Clint had too much to do to stay at the hospital while they were operating on Roper. He told Sister Ruth that he would check back later, then left to go to Kit's Place.

The new doorman passed him through to Dutch, who showed him to Kit's office. There was no conversation between them on the way, which suited Clint.

''How did it go last night?'' he asked Kit. Her men would have reported to her by now.

''Fine,'' she said. ''It was quiet. You have something on your mind?''

''Several things,'' he said, sitting down.

''Would you like a drink?''

''No,'' he said.

''Then perhaps we'd better get to it.''

''Well, for one thing I'm leaving Denver tomorrow.''

''For good?''

''I'm going to go looking for that gold.''

She compressed her lips. ''So you've succumbed to the lure of—''

''I think the man who shot Roper is looking for that gold,'' Clint said, interrupting her. ''If I can find the gold, I'll probably find him.''

She hesitated a moment, then said, ''I'm sorry. That does make sense.''

''I'll keep in touch to see how things are going here.''

''Are we to stay on guard?''

"That's something I think you'll have to decide."

"Why me?"

"Well, not you so much as you and Roper."

"Roper?" she said. "What—"

"He's in surgery now."

"Why didn't you tell me!" she said, standing up quickly.

"Because I didn't want you to go running out of here before we finished talking, like you're about to do."

She stopped herself, but he could see her straining, as if she were on a tether.

"Just give me a few more minutes," Clint said. "He'll be in surgery for a while."

She stood there a few seconds more, then reluctantly forced herself to sit down.

"All right," she said.

"Let's work on the assumption that Roper will survive the operation," Clint said. "He'll still need a guard while he's recuperating. Maybe we'd be better off having the three men alternate, one staying with him at all times."

"You mean, in his room?"

"Yes. You can have Inspector Burns take his man off the door and just put one of your men inside with him. They can stay with him in eight-hour shifts."

She thought a moment, then said, "All right. That's better than having all three staying at the hospital all night long."

"I spoke briefly to Roper," Clint said. "He gave me a starting point to look for the gold."

"How did he know that?"

Clint shrugged. "I don't know," he said. "He's a good detective."

"Did he know who shot him?"

"No," Clint said, "he said it was too dark."

"Oh."

"Will you be able to handle all of this?"

She gave him a pitying look. "What do you think, Clint?"

"I think if you keep your head," he said, "you will be."

"Are you implying," she said evenly, "that because I am a woman I might *not* be able to keep my head?"

"No," Clint said, "I'm implying that because you are emotionally involved you might not be able to keep your head."

"Emotionally—"

"Weren't you just ready to go running out of this room to the hospital?"

She stared at him.

"Tell the truth now."

"All right," she said grudgingly, "all right. Yes, I'll be able to handle things while you're gone. I'll try to keep a tight rein on my emotions. Isn't that the way you would put it?"

He smiled and said, "That's fine."

"What time are you leaving?"

"The train leaves at nine o'clock," Clint said. "Would you like to come and see me off?"

"I don't think so," Kit said. "My guess is that I'll be at the hospital."

"Yes," he said, "that would be my guess as well." He stood up and said, "I'm going to go back to the hospital. Would you like to come along?"

"Yes, why don't I?" she said, standing up. "I've got nothing better to do at the moment."

When they got to the hospital, Sister Ruth showed them where the operating room was.

"How is it going?" Kit asked.

"I don't know," Sister Ruth said. "We'll just have to wait for the doctor to come out."

"Yes," Kit said, "of course."

"I have to go back to the front desk."

"Thank you, Sister," Clint said, touching her arm.

"You're welcome." She started to walk away, then

turned and said, "Oh, there's a friend of yours here."

"A friend of mine?"

"That's what he said. I wasn't sure, so I told him he could wait in Mr. Roper's room."

"What about the policeman?"

"He left when they wheeled Mr. Roper into surgery."

"Did he give you his name?"

"He said . . . Heck. Is that right?"

Clint smiled and said, "That's perfect."

As Sister Ruth walked down the hall, Clint turned to Kit.

"I'm going to Roper's room."

"I'm going to stay here."

"All right," he said. "I'll check back with you."

She nodded and continued to stare at the door to the operating room.

Clint walked to Roper's room. When he entered, Heck Thomas was lying on the bed, his boots hanging over the side.

"Getting some rest?"

"Why not?" Heck said, without taking his head from the pillow. "Roper's not using it."

"He'll want it back, though," Clint said, "after the surgery."

"Oh, I'll be gone by then." He sat up and looked at Clint. "*Will* he be using it again?"

"We hope so."

"At least he woke up," Heck said. "That little sister at the front desk told me that was half the battle."

"The easy half."

Heck took an envelope from his pocket and said, "I thought I'd give you your ticket."

"Thanks," Clint said. "How much?"

"We'll settle up after."

"After what?"

"After we find the gold," Heck said.

"Do you have any idea where to start looking?"

"I just thought we'd start from where the train was hit."

"Have you ever heard of Whiskey Bent?"

"Whiskey what?"

"Whiskey Bent. It's a town in Texas."

"Never heard of it."

"Well, Roper seemed to think that would be a good place to start," Clint said.

"He *told* you that?"

"Yes, before he went in for surgery."

"Did he say why we should start there or how he knew?" Heck asked.

"No, and I don't think we're going to get a chance to ask him."

"Then you think he's going to die?"

"No, but by the time he comes around after surgery, I think we'll be on a train to Texas."

After Heck had left the hospital, Clint went back to the hallway outside the operating room. Kit Russell was seated on a bench just outside the door. She was sitting with her hands flat on the bench on either side of her, staring off into space.

Clint sat down next to her and took her hand. She looked at him and for a moment he thought she might pull away from him, but then she smiled and squeezed his hand hard.

"Hear anything?"

She shook her head. "No, nothing."

They sat there together, holding hands, waiting for somebody to come out and tell them what was going on.

TWENTY-FIVE

Whiskey Bent was a small town.

Heck Thomas and Clint Adams rode down Whiskey Bent's main street. The town seemed to be no more than three blocks long, and some of the buildings looked like they'd been abandoned.

"I hope the livery stable is still in business," Heck said.

Clint didn't comment. He'd been back in the saddle for a full day, and it felt good. As comfortable as riding a train was, it did not give him the same satisfaction as covering ground astride a horse—specifically his big black gelding, Duke.

They found the livery stable, and as they approached it a man stepped out. He was big, with a bulging belly, part of which showed, as his shirt was mostly unbuttoned.

"Help you fellers?"

"Yeah, we'd like to put up our horses," Heck said, dismounting.

"Yeah?" the man said. He studied Duke as Clint climbed down.

"You've got room, don't you?" Heck asked.

"Oh, sure, I've got plenty of room. I ain't never had an animal that good looking in my stable before."

Clint walked right up to the man and said, "He'd better be here when I want him."

The man looked into Clint's eyes, then looked away and said, "Oh, he'll be here, mister. He sure will."

"I wouldn't want you thinking you could sell him out from under me," Clint said. "That would not be a wise thought for you to be entertaining."

"Who, me?" the man said, looking surprised. "I ain't never had a thought in my life."

"Good," Clint said, poking the man in the chest with his forefinger, "keep it that way." Clint turned to Heck and said, "Why don't you take care of this. I'm going to find the telegraph office." He looked at the liveryman and said, "This town does have a telegraph office, doesn't it?"

"Oh, sure, we got a right nice one."

Clint looked at Heck.

"I'll meet you at the hotel."

Heck nodded, and Clint walked away in search of the telegraph office.

When Clint got to the hotel, Heck had already registered them each in a room. He got the key to his room from the desk clerk. He was in his room a few minutes when there was a knock. He opened the door and admitted Heck Thomas.

"So, what's the word from Denver?"

"We'll know as soon as a reply to my telegram comes in," Clint said.

"If we're still here," Heck said. He sat himself down on Clint's bed. "Roper didn't tell you what to look for when we got here, did he?"

"No," Clint said, "just that this would be a good place to start."

"There's nothing around here for miles but flat land," Heck said, "and this town sure doesn't look like it all of a sudden came into two hundred thousand dollars worth of gold."

"Roper must have known something," Clint said. "Somebody must have told him something."

"Yes, but who," Heck said, "and what?"

"I don't know," Clint said. "Maybe if we stay around for a while we'll find out."

"Well, let's get something to eat, anyway," Heck said, standing up. "I'm starved."

Clint agreed and opened the door. They went downstairs, but the hotel dining room was no longer functioning as such. Clint went to the desk and asked where they could get something to eat.

"The saloon," the man replied.

"No restaurant in town?"

"No," the man said, looking at the neglected dining room. "There's not much call for one."

Clint looked at Heck and said, "The saloon."

"Good," Heck said, "I could use a cold beer, too."

They went to the saloon and found it empty except for the bartender.

"What can I get you gents?" the man asked. He was so pleased to have customers, that he was being extra polite and eager to please.

"Can we get a couple of beers?" Clint asked.

"Cold ones?" Heck added.

"Two cold ones comin' up, gents."

When the man set the beers down in front of them, Clint asked, "How about something to eat?"

"Can't offer you anything hot, I'm afraid," the man said. "I do have some dried meats, bread, and some hardboiled eggs."

"Trot it all on out," Heck said. "We'll try and make a meal out of that and anything else you can find."

"Take a table, gents," the man said happily. "Dinner is about to be served."

TWENTY-SIX

The bread was stale and the meat tough. The eggs weren't so bad if they put a lot of salt on them. At least the beer was cold, and it washed everything down. Maybe it wasn't a gourmet meal, but it did ease the hunger pains in their bellies.

When they each had a second beer in front of them, Clint said, "Roper must have had some kind of an informant who gave him the name of this place."

"An informant would have to know more than just the name," Heck said.

"Would have to be someone who was a member of the gang."

"Or someone who witnessed the robbery."

"Or someone who saw what the gang did with the gold *after* the robbery," Clint said. "I have a question for you, since you're the expert."

"What?"

"If the gold was stolen over a month ago, why would the thieves still be around?"

"Do you have any idea how much two hundred thousand dollars in gold weighs?"

"No."

"Neither do I," Heck said, "but you can't put it on the back of a horse, and you can't transport it without attracting attention."

"It would have to be loaded onto a buckboard and covered with a tarp."

"But where would you take it?"

Clint shrugged and said, "You'd have to sell it to someone, turn it into cash."

"Where?"

"You'd have to find a buyer."

"So you would need the buyer first, so that you'd have someplace to take the gold to."

"Then the gold would have to be hidden until they got a buyer," Clint said.

"Hidden where?"

"Where no one would look for it."

They stared at each other for a few moments until Heck said, "Someplace no one from this country could look for it . . . legally."

"Mexico!" Clint said.

"Right!"

They stared at each other again. Clint said, "But *where* in Mexico?"

Heck shrugged and said, "We're back at square one."

"Not quite," Clint said.

"Why not?"

"Because we're here," Clint said, "and Roper had to have had a reason to send us here."

"Sounds like square one to me."

"It isn't," Clint said. "We're here for a reason—we just have to wait for it to become apparent."

Heck finished his second beer. "Can we have another drink while we're waiting?"

"Why not?"

They signaled to the bartender, who was only too happy to bring them each another beer.

"When does this place liven up?" Heck asked.

"It doesn't," the bartender said.

"Do you have a deck of cards anywhere?" Clint asked.

"Behind the bar."

"Toss it over."

The man went back behind the bar and tossed a deck of cards over. Clint caught it one-handed and saw that it was a used deck.

A well-used deck.

He took the cards out and spread them on the table. Some of them stuck together, and he had to pull them apart. He started to shuffle them and found that if he did it slowly he could accomplish it without damaging them any more than they already were.

"Poker?" He said to Heck.

"Why not?" Heck answered, moving his beer aside. "What should we play for?"

Clint thought a moment and then turned to the bartender again. "You got any wooden matches?"

"Sure."

"Bring 'em over."

"How many?"

"All you've got."

The bartender looked surprised, then brought over about a hundred wooden matches in a cigar box. Clint dumped them on the table, split them evenly, and pushed half over to Heck's side of the table.

"What should these represent?" Heck asked, picking one of them up and sticking it in his mouth.

Clint thought a moment, then a smile spread slowly over his face.

"How about the gold? We'll each start with a hundred thousand dollars."

Heck grinned. "Done."

TWENTY-SEVEN

While they played poker a few men wandered in and out, but there were never more than half a dozen people in the saloon at one time, counting them *and* the bartender.

After they had been playing a couple of hours and most of the matchsticks were on Clint's side of the box, there were two men besides the bartender watching the game.

"Bartender," Heck called. "More beer."

"I don't usually drink when I'm playing poker," Clint said.

"It doesn't seem to be affecting your judgment," Heck noted.

The bartender came over, set down the full beers, and removed the empty mugs.

"What have you got left?" Clint asked.

Heck looked down at his matchsticks and said, "About fifteen thousand dollars."

"Well, let's see if we can't make this the last hand," Clint said.

He dealt out a beginning hand of five-card stud, one card down and one card up. Heck had a king of spades, and Clint had a ten of hearts.

"A thousand," Heck said.

"Call," Clint said, "and raise a thousand."

"Call," Heck said.

Clint dealt out the third card. Heck caught another king and Clint a jack.

''Pair of kings,'' Clint said.

''Two thousand,'' Heck said.

''Call,'' Clint said, throwing in the appropriate number of matchsticks.

He dealt out the fourth card: Heck got a queen—no help; Clint got another ten, for a pair.

''Two thousand,'' Heck said again.

''Call,'' Clint said, ''and raise three.''

''Call,'' Heck Thomas said. He had six thousand ''dollars'' left.

Clint dealt the final card: Heck got another king, giving him three; Clint got a jack, giving him two pairs.

''Your bet,'' Clint said.

''Let's just get it over with,'' Heck said, and he pushed in his remaining six thousand dollars, some in whole matchsticks, some in pieces.

''All right,'' Clint said, ''I'll call and raise you five thousand dollars.''

''Where am I gonna get another five thousand dollars?'' Heck demanded.

Clint smiled and pointed. ''In your mouth.''

Heck's eyebrows went up, and he reached for the forgotten matchstick in his mouth.

''Call,'' he said, throwing it into the pot.

''Full house,'' Clint said, showing his jack in the hole.

Heck frowned and turned over his hole card. It matched nothing he had on the table. All he had were the three kings that were showing.

''Congratulations, Clint,'' Heck said, ''you are now the proud owner of two hundred thousand dollars worth of matchsticks.''

''I guess that means I can afford to buy you another beer.''

Clint turned to wave to the bartender, and as he did he noticed that there was only one other person in the saloon, standing at the bar and watching him.

It was a girl.

He signaled the bartender, who brought over two more beers.

"Who is that girl?"

"Her?" the barman said. "Her name is Wendy. She's the town whore."

"*The* town whore?" Heck asked.

"Well, it's not her regular business," the bartender said, "but she's the nearest thing we have. She can be had for a price—sometimes."

As the man walked away, Heck looked across the table at Clint, his eyebrows raised. "A whore who has to be in the mood," he said. "What do you think?"

"Don't look at me," Clint said. "I never pay for a woman."

"Well, I'm not that proud," Heck said, "only she seems to be looking at you."

Clint looked at the girl. She was still looking at him. She appeared to be in her early twenties, dark haired, not pretty but not unattractive. Her body had all the right bumps and curves to it, and her legs—the calves, anyway—were firm.

He looked at Heck Thomas and said, "Make your best move."

"I think I will."

Heck stood up with his beer and walked over to the girl. He talked to her for only a few moments, then came walking back.

"She said no?"

Heck shook his head. "She asked me if your name was Roper."

TWENTY-EIGHT

Clint stood up and walked back to the bar with Heck.

"Are you Roper?" Wendy asked.

Clint could understand her error, if she were comparing him to a description.

"I am."

"Do you have the money?"

"I do."

"Where?" she asked. "Give it to me."

"Not until I get what I want."

She looked around, her glance pausing briefly on the bartender.

"Heck," Clint said.

Heck walked over to the other end of the bar and asked the bartender to go in the back and get him another hard-boiled egg.

"I don't have any made," the man complained.

Heck pinned him with a hard stare and said, "So boil one."

The man averted his eyes only to catch Clint's, then moved out from behind the bar and went into his back-room kitchen.

"The robbers were led by a man named Grissom," she said. "Calvin Grissom."

Clint looked at Heck.

"I never heard of him," Heck said.

"Neither have I," Clint said. "Where is he?"

"Mexico."

"We figured that," Heck said. "Where in Mexico?"

Wendy looked at Heck, then at Clint. "Who is he?" she asked.

"My partner."

"No one mentioned a partner."

"No one mentioned a pretty girl," Clint said.

She lifted her hand to touch her hair, then realized she was betraying the fact that the compliment pleased her and she dropped her hand quickly.

"Where in Mexico?" Heck asked again.

"South."

Heck looked at Clint. "That's a long way to haul that much gold," he said. "Why not just go over the border and find a place?"

"Maybe they already knew where they were selling the gold."

"Do you know anything about that?" Heck asked.

"I don't anything about selling the gold," she said.

"How do you know they're in Mexico?" Clint asked.

"The robbers were here for a week after the robbery," she said. "I slept with many of them."

"How many of them were there?" Clint asked.

"Six," Heck said.

"Five," the girl said at the same time.

Heck looked at Clint and said, "Our information said there were six."

"There were only five," she insisted.

Heck was going to object, but Clint signaled him with a look to keep quiet.

"Where is my money?" she asked.

"How much money are we talking about?" Heck asked.

She looked at Heck and said, "He knows."

"Refresh my memory," Clint said.

Now she stared at Clint and said, "You know—if you're Roper."

Clint didn't say anything.

"You're *not* Roper!" she said, shrinking back from him.

"Roper sent me," Clint said, but she didn't appear to be buying it. Her eyes were darting back and forth, as if she were looking for a chance to run.

Clint looked at Heck and tried to send him a message with his eyes. Heck frowned, but then he seemed to understand and nodded. He also saw that she was primed to run.

"Look, forget it," Heck said. "You'll never convince her that Roper sent you." Heck grabbed her by the arm and squeezed. "Why don't we—"

"Let her go," Clint said.

"Look, she knows," Heck said, squeezing her arm harder and causing her some pain.

"Heck, let her go!" Clint said. He stepped forward and stiff-armed Heck, who staggered back, releasing the girl's arm.

"Hell," Heck said, "if you want her for yourself, be my guest." With that he walked out of the saloon.

"I'm sorry if he hurt you," Clint said.

"Who are you?" she asked.

"My name is Clint Adams," he said.

"Are you after the gold?"

"Yes, but not for the reasons you think. Roper is my friend and somebody shot him to keep him from finding the gold. I want the man who shot him."

"I don't know anything about that," she said.

"But how do you know what you *do* know?"

"I told you," she said. "I slept with them. They talked a lot. You know how men like to brag."

"I guess I do," Clint said, although he couldn't believe that five—or six—men could have been smart enough to pull such a robbery and then dumb enough to talk to a whore about it. There must have been some other way for her to have gotten her information.

"If you're not Roper, then you don't have my money," Wendy said.

"No, I don't," he said. "How much did Roper agree to pay you."

"A thousand dollars."

He wondered if that were true. Any agreement they might have made would have to have been done by telegram, and he hadn't found anything on top of Roper's desk.

"I'm sorry, Wendy," he said, "but I just don't have that kind of money to pay you. All I can promise is that if we do find the gold, I'll see that you get the money from the reward."

"Sure," she said, "a promise from a man. Do you know how much that's worth to me?"

"I'm sorry," he said lamely.

"Can I go now, or do you want to push me around too, like your friend?"

"No, Wendy, I'm not going to rough you up," Clint said. "You can go."

She moved away from the bar slowly, as if she expected him to stop her, and then moved toward the door. When she reached it she darted out, successfully accomplishing her escape.

Clint hoped Heck could follow her without being seen.

When the bartender came out from the back with a hard-boiled egg, Clint took it and ate it with another beer while he waited for Heck to return. He used the now almost worn-through cards to play some solitaire.

"Isn't your friend going to be looking for his egg?" the bartender asked.

"I'll explain it to him," Clint promised.

About twenty minutes after Wendy had left, Heck came walking back in.

"Beer," he said to the bartender. The man drew it and handed it to him. Heck carried it to Clint's table.

"She went to a small shack outside of town," Heck explained.

"And?"

"She's got a man inside, lying in bed. Looks like he's been hurt."

"She insisted that there were only five robbers," Clint said. "I guess we've found number six."

"They must have had a falling out and left number six for dead," Heck said.

"And he decided to get back at them by selling information to Roper."

"How would he know that Roper was involved?"

Clint put down the worn cards and said, "Maybe we should ask him that question."

"Yeah," Heck said, "and a few more."

TWENTY-NINE

Clint followed Heck as he retraced the earlier steps of Wendy.

"She never looked behind her," Heck said on the way. "She bought our act completely."

"Good."

"The shack is just ahead. It's got one window, but you can see the whole inside."

Clint saw the light from the shack ahead. The structure was so badly built that the light literally shone through the walls in slivers. They didn't speak to each other as they approached the shack.

Clint looked in through the dirt-covered window and saw Wendy talking to a man who was lying in bed. He was wearing a shirt but it was open, and Clint could see the bandages around his middle. There was only one door into the shack, and the window he was looking through was the only other way out. The man in the bed did not appear to be in any shape to jump through the window when they came through the door.

Still, Clint signaled Heck to stay at the window while he went around to the door. The only thing he couldn't tell from the window was whether or not the man had a gun. He would go in assuming that he did.

The front door was only a flimsy piece of board. He was about to give it a kick, when he noticed it wasn't locked. He opened it and walked in.

The man on the bed stared at him, and the woman turned and *glared*.

"What do you want?" she demanded.

"I want to talk to him," Clint said.

He saw the man's hand inching toward his pillow.

"You'll never make it to that gun, mister," Clint said.

That arrested the movement of the man's hand.

"Wendy, take the gun out from beneath the pillow and bring it to me."

Wendy looked at the man, who nodded. She slid her hand beneath the pillow, eased the gun out, and handed it to Clint.

The man on the bed was young, about twenty-two. He must have been thin before he was wounded, but now he was almost emaciated.

"What's your name, son?"

"Dave Tanner."

"Dave, tell Wendy to wait outside with my friend."

"Dave—" she started.

"Go on, Wendy," Tanner said. "Let's hear what the man has to say."

She moved to the door slowly, threw a glance at the man on the bed, and then went outside.

"You were the sixth man?" Clint asked.

"Yes."

"What happened?"

"I'm not sure," he said. "I thought it was going to be exciting, but when I saw them kill those two men something happened inside of me. When we got here I tried to take them."

"All of them?"

He nodded. "I figured if I gave the money back and turned them in, maybe I wouldn't go to jail."

"You still would have," Clint said. "Two men were killed."

"Yeah, I know."

"But maybe you wouldn't have gone for as long."

The man shrugged.

"It didn't come to that. I was too slow, and they filled me with lead and left me for dead. Wendy's been taking care of me. I still can't get off this bed, but maybe in a couple of weeks I'll be ready to go to jail."

"Who says you're going to jail?"

The young man stared at him.

"I thought—"

"If you can help us get to the gold and catch the thieves, I don't see any reason why you can't stay right here, with Wendy—if that's what you want."

"It is," David Tanner said.

"Did Wendy tell us everything she knew?"

"Yes."

"South Mexico," Clint said. "That's not much."

"She told you everything *she* knew," Tanner said, "but not everything *I* know."

When Clint left the shack he told Wendy, "You can go back in now."

"You're not going to take him?"

"No."

She started to open the door, then stopped and asked, "Will we be getting any money?"

"Would that make a difference," Clint asked, "between you and him?"

She looked at the shack, as if she could see through it, and then looked at Clint again.

"No," she said, "but it sure would make things a little easier."

"There'll be something," Clint said. "I don't know how much, but there'll be something. I promise."

She nodded and went back inside.

"Whose money did you promise her?"

Clint shrugged. "Roper's."

Heck laughed and they walked away from the shack, back to town.

"What did we get?" Heck asked.

"Grissom," Clint said, "and a town in Mexico called Las Manitas."

"What does that mean?"

"Damned if I know. You can ask when we get there."

"You believe him?"

"Yes," Clint said, "I believe him."

"Let's get some sleep then," Heck said. "We've got a long ride ahead of us."

Before leaving in the morning, Clint checked with the telegraph office and found an answer from Kit Russell in Denver. He was tucking the telegram into his pocket as he exited the office. Heck was outside, standing with both horses. Clint climbed astride Duke as Heck mounted his own horse.

"Well?" Heck asked.

Clint answered without looking at Heck. "He survived the operation."

"And?"

"And he's still alive," Clint said. "Now it's just a matter of time."

"Isn't everything?"

THIRTY

Calvin Grissom looked out onto the main street of Las Manitas. It was a small town that was used for mostly illegal purposes. Thieves from both sides of the border hid out there, and illegal exchanges of money for guns and other such deals were consummated there.

Other things were consummated there, too.

Grissom turned around and looked at the plump Mexican girl on the bed. She had the biggest, softest breasts he'd ever laid his head between. Grissom liked his women big and meaty, and this one, Maria, was a perfect example.

He went back to the bed and slid in next to her. She moved closer to him immediately and covered him with her warmth. He reacted immediately to the touch of her skin, his cock swelling. She felt it and slid down so that she was between his legs. She took his penis between her large breasts and rolled it back and forth, flicking at it occasionally with her tongue.

She had done this to him before and he knew what to expect. She continued to manipulate him between her breasts until he ejaculated, then she dipped her head quickly and took him into her mouth. She sucked him, drawing more from him when he thought he had no more to give. When he was finally drained, she released him with a sleepy, satisfied smile.

She curled up beside him again, then said something to him in Spanish that he could not understand and went to sleep, her big body pressed tightly against him. He didn't speak Spanish and she didn't speak English, but that didn't stop them from enjoying each other.

Grissom thought about the gold, which was on a buckboard, under guard in the livery stable. He and his four partners took turns standing guard over it.

Actually, the other four—Chris Matthews, Bob Josephs, Peter Homes, and Jim Tracy—were not his partners. The robbery was his idea, and he had planned it and called the shots. They *thought* they were his partners, but they really worked *for* him.

He, on the other hand, worked for himself.

They were all in Las Manitas waiting for the people who were going to buy the gold from them. They were getting fifty cents on the dollar, half what the gold was worth, but that was all right.

Grissom had no intentions of sharing it anyway.

THIRTY-ONE

They crossed the Rio Grande just before nightfall and camped. They discussed their plans over a dinner of bacon and beans and coffee.

"If the kid and the girl were telling the truth," Heck said, "we'll have five to deal with."

"If that's the case," Clint said, "we won't have a problem. They're outnumbered."

Heck grinned and said, "Yeah, sure they are. Hey, did you remember to ask that kid how he knew to get in touch with Roper?"

"No, as a matter of fact, I didn't," Clint said. "I'll have to ask him when I bring him and his girlfriend their money."

"How much do you intend to give them?"

Clint shrugged and forked some bacon into his mouth. "Whatever I can pry loose."

"From who?"

"I don't know." Clint grinned and said, "Maybe even from the railroad, huh?"

"Don't expect any help from me on that count."

"Why not?"

"Well, for one thing, the kid went along with the robbery," Heck said. "I don't think he should be rewarded for that."

"What about giving us the information on the location of the gold and the thieves?"

"It still remains to be seen whether or not that information is accurate,'' Heck said, ''but even if it is, he's doing it to get back at them for trying to kill him. He's not doing it for us.''

''Heck, he tried to stop them.''

''And he admits that was only after they killed the two guards,'' Heck said. ''I think you're being too soft on this one, Clint.''

''So you'll go against me if I try to get the money from the railroad?''

''No,'' Heck said, ''but I won't be any help to you, either. I don't have any say in what the railroad does with their money. You'll be on your own if you decide to go ahead with it.''

Clint was unsure of himself now and covered it by taking more food. Was Heck right? Was he being too soft on the wounded gang member? Maybe he should reserve judgment until he saw how good the boy's information was.

''I don't know,'' Heck said.

''What?''

''We could be chasing our tails on this,'' Heck said. ''I mean, the robbery was over a month ago. Even if they did come down here, we're still a good three or four days from this place. They could be long gone by the time we get there.''

''It's possible.''

''And what about you?''

''What do you mean?''

''You're here to find the man who shot Roper,'' Heck said, ''but if he doesn't have the information we have, he sure as hell isn't going to show up in Las Manitas, he's going to still be looking in Texas. You're going in the wrong direction.''

''That may be,'' Clint said, ''but we agreed to do this together. Who knows, the man who tried to kill Roper may be following a different scent that will lead him to the same place.''

"You hope," Heck said. "That would be a pure coincidence, and I know how you feel about that—the same way that I do."

"Not so much of a coincidence," Clint argued. "With as many people as there are looking for that gold, we may run into quite a crowd down there. And if we do, what's going to happen then?"

Heck frowned. "What do you mean?"

"Well, for one thing, who's got jurisdiction here," Clint asked his friend, "Wells Fargo or the railroad? Who gets first call?"

Heck rubbed his jaw, considering the question.

"And if we run into some detectives and bounty hunters who are looking for the gold," Clint continued, "are we going to shoot it out with them? Or will you show them your railroad identification and ask them to go away nice and quiet?"

"I'll do what I have to do to recover the gold for the railroad," Heck said.

"And Wells Fargo will do what they have to do to find the guns who killed two of their men." Clint leaned forward and said, "Heck, we could end up fighting more than just the gold thieves."

"If that's what it takes," Heck said, "that's what we'll do."

With that sobering thought, they cleaned up after themselves and settled down to get some sleep, each alone with his own thoughts.

The only people they'd be able to trust over the next few days were each other.

Or themselves.

THIRTY-TWO

Two days later, late in the afternoon, they rode into a town that did not seem to have a name. There were no signs on the stucco buildings and no town-limits indication.

"What the hell is this?" Heck said.

"A collection of buildings that may or may not be a town," Clint said.

"But what's it called?"

"It doesn't matter what it's called," Clint said, "as long as it has a general store or trading post."

"And a *cantina*."

"And that."

They rode slowly, inspecting each building as they passed it. Most of them seemed abandoned. Finally, more by smell than anything else, they found an inhabited building in which someone seemed to be cooking.

"I don't usually like Mexican food," Heck said, dismounting, "but my mouth is watering."

They had run out of supplies the day before and had only had some water from a waterhole they'd found earlier that day.

Clint dismounted warily, walked around Duke, and put his hand on Heck's arm.

"I don't have a good feeling about this place, Heck," he said.

"Why not?"

Clint shrugged and moved his shoulders, as if a chill had just gone down his back.

"I don't know," he said. "Let's just go easy, all right?"

"Sure," Heck said, "slow and easy. Ain't that the way I always go?"

Clint rolled his eyes and did not reply. They mounted the unsteady boardwalk and entered the building side by side.

From the appearance of the room it *was* a *cantina*. There were tables and chairs, but no one was sitting at any of them. There was a bar, but no one was behind it.

There was the smell of food cooking, and a man and woman could be seen in the kitchen.

"Either there are a lot more people in this town than we think, or these people are expecting a lot of company," Heck said.

"Why would that many people be coming to this town to eat?" Clint asked.

Heck looked at Clint and said, "Because they can't go anyplace else?"

"*Banditos?*" Clint said.

"*Sí*," the woman said.

Clint and Heck both looked at her.

"These people are cooking for a gang of bandits," Heck said.

"And from the looks of those pots," Clint said, "they're due here any minute."

Clint and Heck exchanged a glance.

"I'll get the horses out of sight," Heck said.

"I'll try and reason with these people," Clint said. "Somehow we've got to convince them not to tell the bandits we're here."

"Wait a minute," Heck said.

"What?"

"Who in Mexico would buy the gold from a bunch of *gringos*?"

Clint hesitated a moment, then said, "Revolutionaries!

All they'd have to pay is about half the value of the gold. One hundred thousand dollars."

"They could then turn around and outfit themselves with enough weapons to overthrow ten governments," Heck said. He turned to the couple and asked, "How far are we from Las Manitas?"

They stared at him.

"Las Manitas!" he said again. "Uh, how . . . far? *Quien*—"

"No, that's 'when,' not 'how,'" Clint said. Actually, it was "who."

"Well, how do you say 'how far' in Spanish?"

"It is not necessary, *señor*," the man said.

They looked at him.

"I speak English."

"Well good," Heck said. "Then you've understood everything we've said."

"*Sí*," the man said. "Please, you will help us?"

"Help you? How?"

"As you have surmised, we are cooking for a *bandito* gang. We fear these men. If we did not cook for them and house them when they came here, they would kill us."

"You could always leave," Clint said.

"They would find us," the man said. "They have assured us of that."

"What do you want us to do?" Heck asked.

"Capture them," the man said.

"We're not here to capture *banditos*," Heck said.

"You are here to find gold stolen from your country," the man said.

"How do you know that?" Clint asked.

The man smiled and said, "We understand Spanish much better than we do English. We heard the *banditos* talking about the gold they were going to buy from the *gringos*. With the gold they were going to buy enough guns to overthrow the government."

"You know where the gold is?"

"*Sí*," the man said.

"In Las Manitas?"

The man didn't answer.

"Yeah," Heck said. He looked at Clint, then back at the man. "If we leave now, can we be there by morning?"

The man hesitated, then nodded his head.

"Clint?"

"Right."

Heck looked at the man and his wife. If they left now these people would tell the *banditos* for sure. Heck looked at Clint and knew that he knew that, too.

"Look," Clint said, "we have to leave. We have to get to Las Manitas and wrap things up there before the *banditos* get there."

" 'Wrap things up'?"

"We have to catch them before the *banditos* get there, so we can be ready to catch them," Heck tried slowly. "Do you understand?"

"I understand," the man said. "You do not want us to tell them about you."

"That's right."

"Can we trust you?" Clint asked.

The man looked at his wife. Clint and Heck didn't see anything pass between the two people, but obviously something had. Something that only a husband and wife could see.

"Can *we* trust you?" the man asked.

Clint moved forward and extended his hand. The man hesitated, looked into Clint's eyes, and then took his hand and shook it. He said something in Spanish to his wife, to which she nodded.

"My wife will wrap some food for you."

"*Gracias*," Clint said.

They waited while the woman made two bundles, tied

them, and handed each one. They each said, "*Gracias*," turned, and left.

They left the little no-name town and ate in the saddle, on the way. They would ride all night until they reached their destination.

"So," Heck said, "first we handle the gold thieves, then we take down a band of Mexican bandits."

"That's about the size of it," Clint said.

Heck looked over at Clint and said, "I'm glad we didn't bite off more than we could chew."

THIRTY-THREE

"There it is."

Clint looked down at Las Manitas. There were a lot of lights, and they could hear the sounds of men and women and music.

"They're celebrating," Clint said.

"Let them celebrate."

It was five o'clock in the morning. They had made excellent time. It would be light in half an hour.

"Look at that town," Heck said.

"I'm looking," Clint said.

"Where would you put the gold?"

"In the biggest building in town."

"The livery stable," Heck said.

"Right."

"At the far end of the town," Heck said. "See it?"

"I see it."

"We'll have to leave the horses here and go in on foot."

"Let's circle around and leave the horses on that side," Clint said. "Less chance of the *banditos* seeing them if they get here before we're ready."

"Good idea."

"How many men would you have watching the gold?" Heck asked as they rode.

"Me? I'd have two at least, but from the sound of things I'd say they have one."

"Why?"

"They're deep inside Mexico," Clint explained, "and they have no reason to think anyone knows where they are. All they'd want to do is keep it safe from prying eyes. One man is enough for that."

They continued to circle and stopped when they were south of town.

"All right," Clint said, dismounting. "It all comes down to this."

"Tell me something," Heck said.

"What?"

"We're fairly sure that the gold is down there, and the men who stole it."

"So?"

"Do you really expect to find the man who shot Roper down there also?"

Clint paused, then looked at Heck soberly and said, "No."

"No?"

"I'm starting to think I made a mistake," Clint said. "I don't think anyone has gotten as far as we have. I don't think there are any detectives or bounty hunters within miles of this place."

"Except us."

"Right," Clint said, "except us."

"There it is," the black man said.

The woman looked down at Las Manitas and shook her head.

"Are you sure about this?" she asked.

"No, I'm not," he said, "but then I wasn't sure that you and I could work together, no matter what we had in common."

"I'm still not sure," she said.

He looked at her. "We're here, aren't we, and they're down there?"

"And, hopefully, so is the gold."

"Let's leave the horses here and go in on foot," the black man said.

"The livery stable?"

"That's my guess."

She nodded, and she and her once-reluctant partner started down the hill toward Las Manitas on foot.

They were both *positive* that they were the only two bounty hunters anywhere near this place, and the reward for the stolen gold would soon be theirs.

THIRTY-FOUR

Clint and Heck approached the livery from the rear but were disappointed to find that the building had no rear door.

"We're going to have to go in through the front," Heck said.

"Unless there's a side entrance," Clint said. "You try the right side and I'll try the left."

"All right."

They split up, Clint moving around the left side of the livery. He'd gone halfway when he found a narrow wooden door. He waited there for Heck to find his way back, and when he did he pointed the door out to him.

"I don't see any light under the door," Clint said in a low voice, "but that doesn't mean anything. It could be dark inside, or there could just be one lamp lit. Let's go in very carefully."

"Right."

"I'll go first."

"Why should you go first?" Heck asked.

"Because I found the door."

Heck hesitated a split second, then nodded and said, "That's fair enough."

Clint took out his gun and tried the door. It was unlocked. He guessed that the front doors would be locked. This would be the door they'd use to relieve each other of watch duty.

The door opened soundlessly, which was a surprise. Someone must have greased it recently.

Clint stepped inside. At first it looked dark, but then he saw why. He was on one side of a wagon that was covered with a tarp, and there was a lamp lit, but it was on the other side.

He waved Heck in behind him, then motioned for him to go around the front of the wagon while he went around the back. When Clint reached the back he peered around and saw a man sitting on the ground. There was a lit storm-lamp near him. His legs were spread out, and he had a deck of cards dealt out between them for a game of solitaire.

"Red queen on black king," Clint said, stepping out into view.

The man looked up at him quickly and started to reach for his holstered gun.

"Don't," Heck said.

The man froze.

"It would be healthier just to put the red queen on the black king," Heck said.

The man obeyed.

"Now stand up and put your hands behind your head," Clint said.

As the man stood, Heck moved forward and lifted his gun from his holster.

"All right," Heck said, tucking the man's gun into his belt, "he's defanged."

Clint stepped forward and patted the man down, searching for another weapon and finding none.

"Who are you guys?" the man asked.

"I'm a representative of the railroad you and your friends held up," Heck said.

"Shit."

"You're lucky, friend," Heck said. He pressed the barrel of his gun hard into the man's ribs, making him gasp. "I could be from Wells Fargo. They get real upset when their men are killed."

"I didn't do that," the man said. "That was Grissom."

"Sure," Clint said, "the leader takes all the blame, huh?"

"How did you find us?" the man demanded.

"Let's just say you left a trail," Heck said. "Now, when are you due to be relieved?"

The man hesitated, but Heck dug the barrel of the gun deeper into his side.

"Six o'clock," the man blurted.

"Fifteen minutes," Heck said. "We're in luck. That'll leave just three."

"There's a lot of gold here, fellers," the man said. "I'm sure Grissom would cut you in."

"You got it wrong, friend," Heck said. "We're cutting you and Grissom out." Heck lifted the gun and brought the barrel down on the man's head.

"Let's throw him under the tarp," Clint said, holstering his gun.

"Right."

They lifted the man and hid him on the wagon with the gold.

"We'll take the relief man as soon as he comes through the door," Heck said, and Clint nodded.

They only had to wait five minutes, as the relief man was ten minutes early.

"Hey," he called, coming through the door, but once again Heck lifted his gun, and the man sprawled onto the dirt floor, unconscious.

"Good," Clint said. "Let's tie these two up and go look for the other three."

They were in the act of tying the two men up when Clint heard something.

"What—" Heck started, but Clint quickly lifted his finger to his lips and drew his gun. Heck fell silent and took his own gun from his holster.

"Hold it!" someone yelled, and suddenly the barn seemed more crowded.

Clint turned and found himself facing a big black man pointing a gun at him, just as he was pointing his at the black man.

Heck turned and pointed his gun at a red-haired woman, who was pointing her gun at him.

They were all a hair away from firing.

"Hammer?" Clint said to the black man.

"Clint?" the black man said.

"Clint?" the red-haired woman said.

Clint turned, saw her, and said, "Anne?"

"I feel like a stranger here," Heck said. "Somebody want to tell me what's going on?"

"Jesus," Fred Hammer said, easing the hammer down on his gun. "Clint Adams!"

"What are you doing here?" Anne Archer asked.

"Probably the same thing you are," Clint said.

"The gold?" Hammer asked.

Clint nodded. "This is Heck Thomas," he said. "He works for the railroad."

"There goes the reward," Anne said, holstering her gun.

"Heck, these are friends of mine, Fred Hammer and Anne Archer," Clint said. Heck nodded, mollified now that introductions had been made.

"What are you two doing riding together?" Clint asked.

"We met and discovered we were heading in the same direction," Hammer said.

"The only reason we each knew the other was through you," Anne said.

"We decided that it might be more prudent to ride together."

Clint had worked with either Hammer or Anne on several occasions, but never had he seen them together. Anne usually rode with two other lady bounty hunters, Sandy Spillane and Katy Littlefeather. Hammer usually worked alone.

"Hammer, since when are you a bounty hunter?"

"I'm not, but I heard about this gold and thought I'd give it a try."

"We got lucky and found this place," Heck said, "but how did you find it?"

"One of the thieves has a wife," Hammer said. "We found her."

"He had told her where they would be holed up," Anne added.

"Why did she tell you?" Heck asked.

"That was Anne's doing," Hammer said.

Anne smiled sheepishly. "I pretended that I was a girlfriend of her husband's."

"She got so mad at the guy, she told me where he was," Hammer said, "and here we are. Is this it?" he asked, touching the wagon.

"We assume so," Clint said.

"Let's make sure," Heck said.

The others waited while Heck climbed up onto the flatbed wagon and removed a section of the covering.

"Jesus!" Hammer said.

"God!" Anne said.

Clint was speechless.

They were all looking at gleaming bars of gold. Even by the dim light of the lone stormlamp, it was a blinding sight to behold.

"I've never seen so much gold," Hammer said.

Heck touched it, as if to make sure it was real. He lowered the covering and dropped it down to the floor.

"I want the three of you to know that although the entire reward may not be paid out due to my presence, you won't go unrewarded."

"Well, for one thing, the Wells Fargo reward is still up for grabs," Hammer said.

"Even if that's all we get, it's still a healthy amount," Anne said.

"Split . . . three ways?" Hammer said, looking at Clint.

Clint smiled and held up two fingers. "No, just two ways. I'm in this for my own personal brand of satisfaction."

"That's a lot of satisfaction," the black man said.

"I'll try and get the railroad to kick in with something," Heck said.

"I thought you said you didn't have any control over that?" Clint said.

"I didn't say I didn't have any influence," Heck said, "just that I had no control."

"Well, before we can talk about *any* reward, we've still got things to do," Clint said.

Anne looked down at the two trussed-up men and asked, "How many are left?"

"Three," Clint said.

"Well, that means they're outnumbered," Fred Hammer said.

"Not exactly," Clint said.

Anne and Hammer looked at Clint, and Heck said, "You'd better tell them about the other company we're expecting."

"What other company?" Anne asked.

Clint hesitated a moment, then started telling them about the *banditos* who were on their way to buy the gold.

THIRTY-FIVE

"How many?" Fred Hammer asked.

Clint looked at Heck.

"How many what?" Heck asked.

"How many bandits?"

Heck looked at Clint.

"Did we ask that feller how many *banditos* there were?" Clint asked.

"I'm not sure," Heck said, "but if we did, he might have answered in Spanish."

"That's a good bet," Clint said.

"In other words," Anne said, "you don't *know* how many bandits?"

Clint looked at Heck. "Uh, that's right, we don't."

"But you two were gonna take them on yourselves?" Hammer asked.

"Well, we don't have to now," Clint said brightly. "Now the *four* of us can do it."

"The *four* of us, huh?" Hammer said. "Let me ask you this: Does whether or not we get any of the reward depend on this?"

Clint looked at Heck.

"I would say so," Heck said. "This gold isn't going to be safe while those bandits know about it, and they're not going to go away if we politely ask them to."

Hammer and Anne exchanged a glance.

"What's the limit?" Anne asked.

"What limit?" Heck asked.

"How many bandits do there have to be before we turn and run?" she asked.

"And give up the gold?" Heck asked.

"Yes."

Heck became aware that all three people were watching him, waiting for his answer.

"Maybe the answer is to move it," Clint said.

"Move it?" Hammer repeated.

"Move the gold," Clint said. "Hide it somewhere. If the gold is safe from the bandits, we won't have to face them."

"What about your promise?"

Clint was aware that he had promised the Mexican man and his wife that they would not have to fear the *banditos* any longer.

"We could inform the Mexican government that the bandits are in this area," Clint said. "Let them take care of them. I'll do a lot of things to keep my promises, but dying isn't one of them."

Despite these words, Clint felt badly about his promise.

"I have an idea," Clint said.

"What?" Heck asked.

"First we'll have to round up the other three thieves and secure them and their partners here."

"That sounds like the easy part," Anne said.

"It is," Clint said. "After we've done that, one of us should ride north and try to scout the bandit gang."

"And the rest of us?" Hammer asked.

"We'll have to move this gold and hide it somewhere."

"Where?" Heck asked. "Where do you hide two hundred thousand dollars in gold?"

"Well, if we had the time we could bury it," Clint said.

"We don't know if we have the time or not," Heck said. "And we can't take the chance that those bandits will ride up on us while we're burying it."

''Look,'' Hammer said, ''there are only three thieves left. The four of us aren't necessary. Let me start riding now. Maybe I can find out how many bandits there are and get back here with the information before they arrive. That would give us time to get set for them.''

''Or run,'' Anne said.

''Right on both counts,'' Clint said.

''Well, it sounds all right to me,'' Anne said.

Clint looked at Heck, who nodded.

''All right, Fred,'' Clint said, ''get going.''

''I'll be back as soon as I can,'' Hammer said.

The four of them left the livery together, leaving behind the two trussed-up men. Once outside, Hammer broke away from them and left town.

It was beginning to get light, and the noise of revelry had died down.

''If we're lucky,'' Clint said, ''they're in bed.''

''Maybe even asleep,'' Anne said.

Clint looked at her, and she smiled in mock shyness.

''Anne, you stay here by the livery,'' Clint said.

''What?''

''Just in case one of them gets past us and decides to come and visit his friends,'' Clint explained.

''All right,'' she said grudgingly, ''but if I hear any shooting, I'm gonna come running.''

''That's a deal,'' Clint said. ''Come on, Heck. Let's try and find these weasels.''

''And don't forget,'' Anne said, ''they killed two Wells Fargo operatives.''

''Believe me,'' Heck Thomas said, ''that's not something we're about to forget.''

Clint and Heck, guns drawn, made their way into the center of town. The men in the livery had been subdued before they could be questioned, so they were going to have to find the other three thieves themselves.

As far as Clint was concerned there were three distinct possibilities—the hotel, the *cantina,* or a whorehouse. And if the town didn't *have* a true whorehouse, they'd simply have to find the town whores.

They had one thing in their favor: Neither of them would be recognized as anything but *gringos* who had drifted into town.

Or so they thought.

"There's the *cantina,*" Heck said.

The building was quiet, but the lights were still burning inside, even though the sun was beginning to come up.

"It's still open," Clint said.

Both men took a moment to consider the situation, and then they looked at each other.

"Let's go in and see what we can see," Clint suggested.

Heck nodded. Both men holstered their guns and walked into the *cantina.*

THIRTY-SIX

When they entered, they were surprised.

The place was empty.

They looked around, then at each other, and then around again. There was a beaded doorway in the back wall, which could have led to a kitchen or a back room.

"What do we do now?" Heck asked.

"Let's see if they have any beer."

They started for the bar, when they heard a sound from the back.

A woman's laugh.

A man's laugh.

Heck looked around. "There's no upstairs."

"Just the back," Clint said. "There must be rooms back there."

Heck backed up and looked outside, then moved back inside again and drew his gun.

"Let's do it."

Clint drew his gun, and both moved toward the beads. Clint spread them to step through, and Heck followed. They were in a long hallway. There was a door on the right wall, a door on the left, and a door all the way at the end. They stood stock still and listened. When the laughter came again, it seemed to be coming from the far door. Clint pointed. Heck nodded, and they started down the hall.

Each paused briefly to put an ear to the door on either side, then continued down the hall. They stopped outside the door and listened. The sounds had changed from laughter to heavy breathing and creaking bed springs.

Then they heard a man groan.

A woman moan.

And a man grunt.

Heck frowned, and Clint shook his head.

It sounded to them like two different men.

The door was flimsy. Whether it was locked or not, they decided to kick it in. The element of surprise would work in their favor.

Clint stepped back and Heck stepped aside. Clint kicked the door just below the doorknob, and it flew open. Heck stepped into the room first, with Clint right behind.

On the bed the three people turned their heads to see what was happening. The woman was in the center, and she seemed to be linking the two men together.

Both men turned and reached for their guns, which were hanging on the bedposts.

"Don't!" Clint shouted.

Both men froze. The woman between them didn't seem to know what to do, so she froze also.

Clint and Heck heard a door open behind them. Clint kept his eyes on the men and woman on the bed. Heck turned quickly as a man stepped out into the hall, holding a gun. When he saw Heck, surprise registered on his face. He raised his gun, but Heck shot him in the chest. Heck went down the hall to make sure he was dead, then returned.

"Just one," Heck said to Clint.

"The two in the barn, and these two—that makes five," Clint said.

"Five what?" the girl on the bed asked.

Clint looked at her and said, "Five *dead* men, if your . . . friends don't do as they're told."

She stared at Clint for a long moment and then said, "Could we move? These fellers aren't even hard anymore, and this is really getting uncomfortable."

"Just a moment," Clint said.

Heck moved forward and removed both guns from the bedposts, then went back and stood next to Clint.

"Now you can all get up."

The girl actually pushed the man in front of her away from her and scrambled to the end of the bed. She stood up, tall and naked, obviously American and not Mexican.

She rubbed her hands over her firm buttocks and, being alone in a room with four men, could not help preening for them. She thrust her chest out, and all four men found themselves looking at her impressive breasts.

"You'd better get dressed, miss," Clint finally said.

"Let's not be in such a hurry," Heck said, but Clint knew he was kidding—at least he hoped he was.

The men watched her as she dressed, and on her way out she said, "I have a room in the hotel, in case you get lonely later."

"I'll keep it in mind," Clint said.

As she walked down the hall, one of the men asked, "Can *we* get dressed?"

"I don't think so," Clint said. He looked at Heck. "What do you think?"

"No," Heck said, "I don't think so."

"You can't leave us here like this," one of the men said.

"Sure we can," Heck said with a smile.

"Which one of you is Grissom?" Clint asked. "Or was that him?" He indicated the dead man in the hall.

"I'm Grissom." It was the man who had complained about being naked. He was a tall, well-built man, in his late thirties. The other man was a few years older, taller and almost painfully thin. Clint looked at the huge thing hanging down between his legs and wondered how the woman had survived.

"On second thought," Clint said, "maybe we should let them get dressed."

"All right," Heck said.

"Gentlemen," Clint said, "we are going to have company very soon and we have some talking to do before they arrive."

"Before who arrives?" Grisson asked. "And who the hell are you two?"

"We'll talk after you get dressed, Grissom—unless, of course, you and your friend *prefer* to walk around naked."

Grissom frowned unhappily and said, "We'll get dressed—but after that I want some answers."

"For that," Heck Thomas said, "you'll have to say the magic word."

"What magic word?"

Heck pointed the barrel of his gun at Grissom and said, "Please."

"You're lying," Grissom said.

"Sure I am," Clint said.

Clint, Heck, Grissom, and his friend, whose name was Jim Tracy, were sitting at a table in the *cantina*.

"What do we gain from lying?" Heck asked.

"If a gang of bandits was on its way here, you wouldn't be here," Grissom said, and his friend nodded.

"I'm not going anywhere without the gold, friend," Heck said.

"Neither am I . . . friend," Grissom said.

"Or without you," Heck said, grinning, "and let's not forget who has the gun."

Grissom gave Heck a pained look and then looked at Clint.

"What do you want from us?"

"A little help."

Grissom laughed. "You kill one of my men, tie up two more, you're gonna take the gold away and put us behind bars, and you want *us* to help *you*?"

"Actually, in helping us you'll be helping yourselves," Clint said.

"How?" Grissom asked.

"To do what?" Tracy asked.

Clint looked at Tracy and said, "To stay alive."

"You can't pull that on us," Grissom said.

"Pull what?" Clint asked.

"Those bandits are coming here to meet us," Grissom said. "Why would they kill us?"

"Have they ever seen you?" Clint asked.

"No."

Heck shrugged and said, "One *gringo* pretty much looks like another."

"What does that mean?" Tracy asked.

Grissom looked at Tracy. "It means we're going to help these gents arrange a little reception."

Tracy looked at Grissom, then at Heck and Clint, and then back at Grissom. "Does that mean we don't get the gold?"

THIRTY-SEVEN

They put the remaining four thieves to work.

Clint took two of them—including Grissom—and Anne and began to set up a reception for the *banditos,* while Heck took the other two and moved the gold.

"You've got an admirer," Anne said to Clint at one point.

"What?" Clint asked, not taking his eyes off the two men.

"Second window from the left," she said. "The hotel."

He risked a look and saw the whore who had been with Grissom and Tracy watching him from the window.

"A friend?" Anne asked.

"She was with Grissom and Tracy when we busted in," he explained.

"Ooh," Anne said, "you must have seen a lot of her."

"Enough."

"She invite you up?"

"Why do you ask that?"

"She's got the look of a woman who invited you up."

"Only if I get lonely."

"Well," Anne said, "with what we're waiting for, that doesn't seem very likely in the near future, does it?"

"No, it doesn't."

"Hey!" one of the man called out. His name was Chris Matthews.

"What?"

"When we're finished digging holes and those *banditos* get here, are we gonna get our guns back?"

"Hey, friend," Clint said, "do I look that dumb? Keep digging."

The man gave him a cold look and then went back to his digging.

"Is this going to work?" Anne asked Clint.

"Well," Clint said, "that really depends on you, doesn't it?"

"I guess it does."

"How good is your timing?"

"You can ask me that?" she asked. "Look where I picked to meet up with you again."

When the preparations were finished, they herded the four thieves into the *cantina*.

"Does this town have a jail?" Clint asked Grissom.

"Hell, no."

Clint looked at Heck. "We've got to find someplace to lock them up."

"Why not just give us our guns?" Grissom asked. "You're gonna need the help."

Clint looked at Grissom and said, "Thanks, but you fellers have done enough."

"Eight guns are better than three," Grissom said.

"Thanks," Clint said again, "but we'll have four." He looked at Heck and said, "Hell, let's just tie them up and put them in that back room."

Heck said, "Let's just tie them up and put them in *separate* rooms."

"Good idea."

Clint and Heck were coming from the back of the *cantina* when they saw Anne standing at the front door.

"Hammer's riding in," she said.

"Good," Clint said. "Better have him hide his horse and then bring him in here. We've got to go over this."

As Anne left the *cantina*, Heck looked at Clint and said, "Well, it'll be nice to know what we're going up against, won't it?"

A few minutes later Anne returned with Fred Hammer, who looked agitated. After a wave from Clint the bartender—who was just as frightened of *these gringos* as he was of the *first* group—drew a cold beer and extended it to Hammer. He took a moment to drink down half of it before turning to face Clint, Heck, and Anne.

"They're about an hour behind me," Hammer said. "They're not traveling in any great hurry."

"How many?" Heck asked.

"Twenty-five, as near as I can figure," Hammer said. "I may be off one or two either way."

"Twenty-five," Clint said, looking at Anne and Heck. "It could be worse."

"It could always be worse," Heck said.

Hammer finished his beer and asked the bartender for another one.

"I see you've rigged the street," he said, holding the second beer.

Heck looked at him sharply, then at Clint, and then back at Hammer.

"You *noticed* that?"

Clint touched Heck's shoulder and said, "I'd have been disappointed if he hadn't."

"It shouldn't be noticeable," Hammer said, "not to a bunch of *banditos*."

"I sure hope not," Heck said. He looked at Anne Archer and said, "Forgive me, but if it is, we're going to be royally fucked."

"Heck," Clint said, "I don't remember your vocabulary being so . . . progressive."

THIRTY-EIGHT

An hour later they were in position.

Fred Hammer was on the roof of a building that would put him on the *banditos*' left when they rode into town.

Anne Archer was directly across the street from Hammer but on the ground. Hers was the key position. Everything depended on her timing—and on how well the street had been rigged.

Heck Thomas was the ground, across the street from Anne. Once the *banditos* were in position, he would move in behind them, cutting off their escape.

"Think you can do that alone?" Clint asked.

Heck thought a moment. "Is there a shotgun in town?"

"We'll find one."

"I can do it."

Clint turned to Anne then.

"Are you all set?"

"All set."

"Just remember, count twenty from the time I take off my hat."

"Right."

He started to turn away, then looked back at her.

"There's something I've never asked you before."

"What's that?" Anne asked.

"You can count to twenty, can't you?"

"Are you kidding?" she asked. "I can count to a hundred."

"Well, do me a favor," Clint said. "Don't get carried away. Stop at twenty."

She wrinkled her nose at him and said, "Just for you, Clint."

Clint turned to Hammer, who held up his hands and said, "Whoa, I can't count."

Clint waved his hand and said, "Just start shooting when all hell breaks loose."

Hammer grinned, his teeth showing very white against his ebony skin.

"And don't fire without hitting something."

"I kin do that, Massah!"

"I was confident that you'd be able to. All right, I think we're set here."

They all took up their positions and waited for Hammer to sing out. He had the highest vantage point and would sound the alarm when the *banditos* were coming.

The streets of Las Manitas were even more deserted than usual. That is, there still weren't any people on the streets, but they *felt* deserted rather than being just empty.

Clint was in his position in front of the *cantina*. When the *banditos* rode into town his task was to step out into the street, directly in front of them, to try and talk them into leaving.

Performing the task was easy.

Living through it was going to be the hard part.

THIRTY-NINE

"This is it!" Hammer called out.

Clint looked up, and Hammer waved from the roof. He exchanged glances with both Anne and Heck, then checked the street one last time to make sure everything was in place.

He stepped down off the boardwalk and waited.

He heard them before he saw them. The sound of their horses approaching increased until finally they entered the street, twenty-five dirty, sweaty Mexicans wearing clothing that was once white, bandoliers crisscrossing their chests, most of them smoking cigars.

These guys were actually trying to look like *banditos*.

As they rode down the street, Clint waited until they were in the right position, then walked deliberately into the center of the street.

The *banditos* approached and stopped about fifteen feet from Clint. The leader took a cigar out of his mouth and dropped it into the street. It was now the only thing that made him look different from the rest.

"*Señor*," the man said, "you are blocking our way."

"In more ways than one," Clint said.

The man frowned.

"What do you mean?" the *bandito* leader asked. "Are you the *gringo* with the gold to sell?"

"I am the *gringo* with the gold," Clint said, "but I don't want to sell it."

The man frowned. "I do not understand." He waved his arms to take in all of his men and said, "We came here to do business for the gold, and now you say you do not wish to sell?"

"That's right."

"You are perhaps trying to raise the price?"

"No," Clint said, "I just don't want to sell."

"This is not right," the man said, frowning.

The man on his right asked, "*¿Que pasa?*" and the leader took a moment to explain.

"My *compadre* does not understand either."

"Let me explain," Clint said. "You see, I am not the man you came here to do business with."

"I see," the *bandito* said. "Well then, where is he?"

"I killed him."

The man took a moment to think about this, then asked, "You took the gold from him?"

"Yes."

"But not to sell it?"

"No."

"Then *señor*, why did you take the gold?"

"To take back to the United States and return it to the railroad."

"The railroad?"

"It was stolen from the railroad," Clint said, "and I intend to return it."

The *bandito* thought about that for a few moments, then began to laugh. He turned and said something to the rest of his men, who also began to laugh.

The leader turned back to Clint and said, "*Señor*, it is good that you killed the man who had the gold. Now we will take the gold from you, instead of him."

"You can't take the gold, *señor*," Clint said. "I'm taking it back to the United States."

"By yourself, *señor?*" the man asked, laughing. "All by yourself?"

"No," Clint said, "not by myself."

"You mean you have help, *señor*?"

"That's right," Clint said, "I have help."

"How much help, *señor*?"

"Enough."

"Enough?" the man repeated. He leaned forward in his saddle and said, "Enough to handle all of us, *señor*?"

Clint didn't respond.

"Where is the gold, *señor*?"

Clint took off his hat and said, "That's none of your business. Now I suggest you and your men turn around and leave."

. . . nine . . . ten . . . eleven . . .

"Not without the gold, *señor*," the bandit leader said, drawing his gun.

. . . twelve . . . thirteen . . . fourteen . . .

"Where is it?"

Clint put his hat back on and just shook his head at the man.

. . . fifteen . . . sixteen . . .

Clint watched the man closely, wondering if he should have told Anne to count to fifteen.

"You will tell us where the gold is, *señor*," the man said, "or we will kill you and find it."

. . . seventeen . . .

"You wouldn't find it."

. . . eighteen . . .

"Then you will tell us."

"No, I won't."

"Yes," the man said, grinning, "you will."

. . . nineteen . . .

He waved an arm, and two of his men began to dismount.

"Where is all your help, *señor*?" the leader asked.

. . . twenty!

"Just wait," Clint said.

The two men who had dismounted started toward Clint.

Twenty was too long, he thought, and then the first charge went off.

There had been no dynamite in town, but there had been gunpowder. Clint had had the thieves dig ditches in the street—small trenches, actually—and filled them with gunpowder. Then he'd had them dig holes, which had been filled with enough gunpowder for a small explosion, mixed with nails from the hardware store.

It had been Anne's job to light the fuses, hopefully when all of the bandits' attention was on Clint.

One man had heard a sizzling sound and had looked down in time to see a puff of smoke moving beneath his horse. He'd opened his mouth to say something to his leader, and that was when the first charge went off.

As the explosion sounded, Clint threw himself to the ground. He was the only one of his people who was vulnerable to the blasts, and even as he moved he felt the pain in his left arm as something hit him.

As he hit the ground, he heard the cries of pain as the nails flew into the air, propelled by the explosions, and tore into the bandits.

From behind them, Heck Thomas began to fire into the confusion. Men were falling from horses, and the animals themselves were reeling in pain and panic from the nails and the explosions.

The second charge went off, and Hammer began to fire down into the crowd. Anne Archer also opened fire from her vantage point on the ground.

By the time the third and last charge had gone off the bandits were all dismounted and their horses were scattered. Heck Thomas had to duck several panicked horses, who might have ridden over him.

Clint got up on one knee after the final blast and surveyed the damage. At least half the bandits were lying flat on the ground and half of the others were either sitting on the ground or down on one knee, bleeding.

Clint stood up and walked over to the leader, who was one of those sitting on the ground. He looked up at Clint, his eyes glazed, blood running down both sides of his face.

"See?" Clint said to the man. "I had enough help."

EPILOGUE

"Where have you been?" Anne Archer asked.

Clint walked up to her table in the Denver House dining room. She and Clint had been in Denver since the day before.

They had spent the night in the same room, in the same bed, making love and talking about what they would do with their share of the reward money. . . .

"Well," she said, her hand stroking his penis, "of course I have to split mine with my partners."

"Ah, Sandy and Katy," Clint said. "How are they?"

"They're fine," she said, kissing his chest. "They send you their love."

She had sent them a telegram upon their arrival in Denver.

She rolled on top of him, and he slid his hands down her back to cup her firm buttocks.

"What are you going to do with yours?" she asked.

"I have to split mine, too," he said.

"With Roper?"

"Yes."

She kissed his mouth and said, "You're a nice man."

"He got me involved in the first place."

"Well, at least Heck's not taking a share," she said.

"As an employee of the railroad he can't."

"Why not take a piece of the Wells Fargo money?"

Clint shook his head and said, "He said there were too many people splitting that already."

Clint, Anne, and Hammer would each get a piece of that, as well as Wendy and the sixth outlaw in Texas, as would Roper. Of course, they'd be getting theirs from Clint's piece.

"I'll put mine in the bank," Clint said. "After cutting it this way and that, there won't be that much left to do much else with."

"What about Roper?"

"He's fallen on hard times," Clint said. "He says it was just one of those things. His share should help him out, maybe get him back on his feet."

"Well, it sounds like everyone will be happy," Anne said.

"I guess."

"You don't sound so enthused."

"I'm just not sure my share is worth the trouble I had to go to," he said.

"Well, maybe I can make it worth your while," she said.

She kissed his nipples, then moved her mouth down over his belly until she had the head of his penis between her lips. She licked it, wetting it thoroughly, then took it into her mouth, cupping his testicles. As she took more and more of him into her mouth he closed his eyes, reached down and cupped her head, and gave himself up to her avid ministrations. . . .

"I missed you this morning," Anne said now.

"I wanted to go and see Roper."

"How is he?"

"They'll be letting him out of the hospital soon," Clint said, sitting down across from her.

"That's good."

"There was some other news, too."

"What?"

"They found out who tried to kill him."

"Who?"

"The policeman, Burns."

"Why?"

Clint shrugged. "The inspector is not talking. They caught him making another try at Roper in the hospital. Apparently Burns didn't like the idea that Roper was recovering."

"Who caught him?"

"Kit Russell's men," he said. "She'd kept them guarding him even after I left."

"And it had nothing to do with the gold?"

"Nothing," Clint said. "Roper had just gotten the telegram about the gold a couple of days before and was clearing the decks to leave Denver."

"Coincidence," she said. "I know how much you hate that."

"Well, it exists," he said, "once in a while."

"Oh," she said, "this came for you this morning." She handed him a telegram.

He took it and read it.

"It's from Heck. The money should be here by tomorrow." He folded it up and put it in his pocket.

"What will you do then?" she asked.

"Well, after I send Hammer his share, I'll head back to Texas. What about you?"

"Sandy and Katy will be waiting for me in Wyoming."

"On somebody's trail?"

"Naturally," she said. "You know, I wonder whatever happened to Jake Benteen. Wasn't he supposed to be on the trail of the gold?"

"That's what I heard," Clint said. "Maybe he just never got headed in the right direction."

"It would have been nice to meet him," she said. "He's sort of a legend in my business."

"Jake's a legend, all right. Maybe after this he'll give

up gold hunting and go back to hunting men.''

''Shall we order breakfast?'' she asked.

Clint was about to answer when he saw Ellie Lennox enter the dining room.

''Would you mind if we had someone join us?'' Clint asked.

Anne turned and looked at the woman in the doorway. ''Friend of yours?''

''I think so,'' he said. ''I'll have to make sure, though.''

''Well, you go and make sure, and I'll order coffee.''

He touched her hand in thanks, then got up and walked over to Ellie to find out if they were still friends.

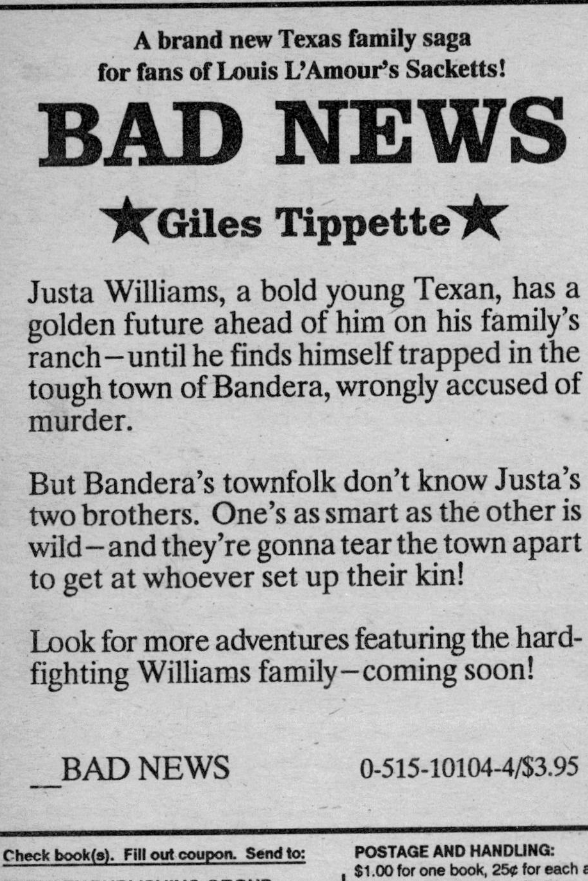
A brand new Texas family saga
for fans of Louis L'Amour's Sacketts!
BAD NEWS
Giles Tippette
Justa Williams, a bold young Texan, has a golden future ahead of him on his family's ranch–until he finds himself trapped in the tough town of Bandera, wrongly accused of murder.
But Bandera's townfolk don't know Justa's two brothers. One's as smart as the other is wild–and they're gonna tear the town apart to get at whoever set up their kin!
Look for more adventures featuring the hard-fighting Williams family–coming soon!
__BAD NEWS 0-515-10104-4/$3.95